DA BROWN

Recycled Virgin

I0718544

First published by Somewhat Grumpy Press Inc. 2020

Copyright © 2020 by DA Brown

All rights reserved. No part of this publication may be reproduced, stored or transmitted in any form or by any means, electronic, mechanical, photocopying, recording, scanning, or otherwise without written permission from the publisher. It is illegal to copy this book, post it to a website, or distribute it by any other means without permission.

This novel is entirely a work of fiction. The names, characters and incidents portrayed in it are the work of the author's imagination. Any resemblance to actual persons, living or dead, events or localities is entirely coincidental.

DA Brown asserts the moral right to be identified as the author of this work.

DA Brown has no responsibility for the persistence or accuracy of URLs for external or third-party Internet Websites referred to in this publication and does not guarantee that any content on such Websites is, or will remain, accurate or appropriate.

Designations used by companies to distinguish their products are often claimed as trademarks. All brand names and product names used in this book and on its cover are trade names, service marks, trademarks and registered trademarks of their respective owners. The publishers and the book are not associated with any product or vendor mentioned in this book. None of the companies referenced within the book have endorsed the book.

Fall 2022 printing
1st edition ISBN: 978-1-9992884-2-6

Second edition

ISBN: 978-1-7380743-2-7

This book was professionally typeset on Reedsy.
Find out more at reedsy.com

"Only a Woman, divine, could know all that a woman can suffer."

— Willa Cather, Death Comes for the Archbishop

"Think about the whole Biblical story of Mary. She wakes up and sees something with a lion, eagle, and human face that wants to inseminate her with the Holy Seed. She's practically a saint just for not killing herself on the spot."

— Thomm Quackenbush, Flies to Wanton Boys

Contents

Acknowledgement

I've been honoured to have the help of so many with this first novel. From its first creation during the 3DayNovelContest, through editing and readings by, among others, Tim Covell, Judy Kennedy, Sylvie Spraakman, Heather Loney, Emily Beresford, and Fred Casey, and the support of the Darksiders Writing Group, there have been many hands helping smooth this into shape. They've caught inconsistencies and added to my characters, and made this book a better thing. Of course, they are not to blame for any of the content and all the errors are my own.

I am also indebted to a course in Mariology from the Atlantic School of Theology for additional insights. AST is a surprisingly welcoming environment for people questioning faith. I am grateful for their tolerance. They are not to blame for this book, but have been supportive of my desire to write it. Please check out their website at: http://www.astheology. ns.ca/home/welcome.html

Finally, I'm thankful for my Roman Catholic upbringing. Though I've strayed, the rich background and history of the church have informed my entire life.

Cover: *St. Editha and the Nuns of St. Mary* (1959P41), by Thomas Matthews Rooke, after Ford Maddox Brown, 1908. Photo by Birmingham Museums Trust, licensed under CC0.

1

Halifax

Ten in the morning on a damp fall day in Halifax, Nova Scotia. Not an auspicious start, Marian thought, as she dragged her wet sneakers across campus. She had been hoping for some celestial sign that she'd made the right choice, that she should be here, now, but feeling the rain soak through her brown hair to her chilled scalp wasn't sending her a positive message. The rain fell harder, and she tugged up her hood. She craved a warm cup of coffee, a wool blanket and a good book, maybe even a roaring fire.

No hope for that. She was on a mission. It was time for Marian's Introduction to Christianity class, and she had no idea where to find the seminar room. She ran through puddles to the big old building that looked like it should be a part of the college, only to find it closed up, chains across the door handles. Turning on her heel, she splashed mud up her pants legs, soaking them through. She stomped, furiously wet, across to the newer block-shaped building. The wind slapped her face like an insult.

At least she found the right place. An impossibly young

man wearing a "Can I Help You?" button pointed her down the hallway and she squelched gratefully towards the chatter of students. She slopped into the classroom and tugged her rain slicker off, sprinkling the other students with water. Apologizing in all directions, she handed out slightly damp tissues. No one answered her. They were all busy wiping themselves and their laptops dry. One girl, her black hair done up in braids, smiled a tiny smile. Her pigtails were dripping.

"Meet your classmates" time and already she felt so out of place, wordless. The clouds hung low over the harbour and Marian couldn't stop staring out the window at them as they rolled. They matched her thoughts. The students were unwelcoming. She was much older than all of them. Most of all, she had no credible explanation for why she had come to this place. Coming to herself with a shock, she realized the class was staring at her.

The professor, the tall, bewhiskered and threatening Dr. Rutgers, had asked the class to state their names and explain what they expected to learn. His appearance did nothing to help her anxiety. Something about him recalled the Blake version of God, backed by lightning and punishment.

Marian ran her fingers through her hair while she tried to think of an answer. It was greasy after her desperate flight. No time to wash when making a getaway. Now it was greasy and disgustingly wet, lying in fishy tendrils down her back. The classroom silence stretched. The tall student in the corner coughed a moist cough. Averting her head from the water droplets, Marian blurted out, "I'm Marian Steeves. I'm not sure quite why I'm here." She kicked the table leg in front of her, frustrated by her bland replies. "I think I'm interested in learning more about religion, but I have no idea what I want to do with the information."

Dr. Rutgers blinked at her, his face blank. "Why not?"

"How much of all this is real? What is religion good for? Does God exist? Why are there so few women?"

Dr. Rutgers scanned the classroom. Over eighty percent of the class was female. He waggled his prodigious eyebrows at her.

"Well, that's interesting, too," said Marian. "So many women here in class, and so few there?" She pointed at the large Bible the prof had on his desk. "What's that about?"

Dr. Rutgers peered at her over his glasses. "Yes, hmmm," he responded. He pushed his glasses up his nose. "Next…"

Marian slumped down in her seat as the other students introduced themselves. For a moment she was sure she'd seen a flicker of interest in Dr. Rutger's eyes and it had given her encouragement. Now she wasn't sure. She wondered if she was too late to withdraw. Maybe she could get a refund. She had only decided to study here on a whim, right?

Mentally, she shook her head. She couldn't return to New Brunswick, she just couldn't. Not to Moncton, not to her husband, not to any of it. The scholarship from the Atlantic School of Theology allowed her to escape here, to Halifax. She'd already paid her small savings for the classes, used the scholarship for residence. All gone now. She was trapped.

Still, she sensed good things about this place. The school was located on the very edge of the sea, the protected harbour opening outwards to the entire world. Escape was possible. It seemed all of the classrooms could view sky or ocean, giving her mind a place to rest. The library had a spectacular study room surrounded in windows that she'd dashed up to investigate when she first arrived.

The school appealed to her sense of history, too, spoke to her in so many ways. Apparently there had been theological teaching on the same spot since 1878. Marian couldn't help but feel that, if she was looking for answers, this history of discussion and thought might be a place to dig for them. Good spirits. Plus, they said the school was 'ecumenical.' That intrigued her, given her mixed religious background. She had wondered if that meant there would also be room to discuss religions other than Christianity, but when she looked at the required classes it appeared that wasn't a first-year option.

Listening to fellow students as the introductions stumbled around the room, she guessed they might not care so much about that broader view. The rest of the class, mostly white, mostly fresh out of college, stated their names and their burning desire to be a minister or the next best thing. They smiled beatifically, faces inoffensive and trying to look chosen, and nodded to each other. Everyone seemed so sure, so convinced. Marian felt like she was back in high school and not with the in crowd. Next thing, she thought, they'll be having pyjama parties and not inviting me.

So much for finding kindred spirits. Her classmates looked scary, except for one tall brown guy, who, when it was his turn, mumbled something incoherent about "searching."

Dr. Rutgers snorted at him. "Searching? For what?" He pointed at the student's carefully frothed cappuccino. "More caffeine? Beer? Religion a la carte? Women?" The guy cringed. Marian felt sorry for him. Why was he under attack?

He and Marian glanced at each other, eyes wide. Were they the only ones with questions? She made a mental note to meet him for coffee, and wrote down his name in case they missed each other. Albert Clayton. She hoped they'd be sharing more classes. It sounded like they could use each other's support.

Albert hovered at the doorway at the end of class and Marian's heart lifted. It looked like he also wanted to talk with her. As she made a beeline to the exit, Dr. Rutger called out to her. His was not a voice to ignore. She sighed, waved a brief goodbye to Albert, and turned back. Friendship would have to wait.

"Marian," he began, "I have an unusual idea for your community project."

She wilted. More work, and she was just hanging on as it was. It had taken such an effort to sneak out from her husband's muscled grip and flee. She was still tired. Unwashed. Not ready for prime time.

Wasn't studying theology supposed to be restful? And easy, especially for her. After all, she had experience. That had been her plan. Escape Moncton, get an easy degree, find a job, hide.

She had hoped that, as a mature student, she could opt out of the community placement. Of course, that was before she saw her classmates. Some of them were her 'maturity' times two or more. So what would they have her do? Could she get out of it if she pleaded? Tears, would tears work? She squeezed her eyes shut experimentally.

"All the students attend community placements," Dr. Rutgers growled, as if reading her mind. "I sense a ministry posting mightn't agree with you. How about volunteering at the Compass program?"

Marian pretended to look interested. "What's that?"

"It's a program for mothers and babies whose partners are in trouble with the law. Sometimes there's been abuse. There's always poverty. The group helps the women get through pregnancy and their babies' first months safely, with food support, friendships and health information. The local group of churches partner with Public Health to offer it. We hope it helps the women become stronger, stand up for themselves, get their lives in order. Direct them a bit. They could use you."

"Why me?"

"You've seen your classmates. How many of the ones with any life experience could do the bending and lifting? There are boxes of food to carry, babies to look after. Plus, you seem to more closely relate to the godless."

"What?" Marian blanched.

Dr. Rutgers looked at the floor, shrugged. "Yes, well, the group is not at all receptive to preaching or evangelizing. The previous student was, ah, promptly shown the door. I believe they pitched her Bible after her. Fortunately, there were no serious injuries."

Marian goggled at him. "You are sending me to a group of violent women? Fantastic."

"They aren't violent, exactly. They are more the 'show me' types. You are an adult with practical life experience, and, from your application to the school, not a fan of evangelizing. Plus, the coordinator needs help. The group is a victim of its own success. It gets bigger every week."

Marian wondered what she put in her application that made Dr. Rutger think she had 'safe for dangerous situations' and 'will not evangelize' labels stuck to her back. She'd played the helper role already, thanks. More than a few times. She worked with women and families so often, experienced the heartbreak and failure of that. The thought of doing it again with a set of potentially violent people gave her the shivers.

Why did women, or more specifically, Marian, always have to help in places where no one else would? Feeling like a sucker, she took the number of the contact person for the group from Dr. Rutgers, and pushed her way out through the old oak doors. Another midwife-type post. How many generations had she already served? Twenty-five? Thirty? When would it be enough?

2

Back to School

Her next class was on resurrection. She was extremely keen to learn about that. Or explore it, anyway. The prof, a chewed-string woman with bad teeth and a tendency to lisp, only chose to teach about THAT resurrection. And the Virgin Mary's. Apparently, no one else ever resurrected in her Bible. Adding insult, she described the end of Mary's life as more of a vacuuming into the heavens than a true rebirth. Marian stopped listening in exasperation and did her readings for the next class. She fought the urge to make quiet vacuuming noises to herself between pages. She was getting punchy.

The day oozed by, with Marian feeling more and more alien. Every class was for believers, not questioners. Albert kept crossing his legs and jiggling his foot, which was driving her crazy. The two of them had seated themselves closer and closer together as the day progressed. Now they were side by side, and he was making her writing go all squiggly. She tapped his leg to make him stop. He did, for a moment or two, and then he was right back at it. She gave up.

"Wow," he whispered during the break in the lecture, 'Theocracy in the early Christian church.' "Do you think they'll roast us on a cleansing fire us when they figure out we don't quite buy all of this?"

"Don't know, but I plan to carry salt everywhere with me, just in case I need protection," Marian said. "I can't help wondering if I should even be here."

"Oh no. Don't you dare leave. I'll wither, unbelieving all by myself. That wouldn't be fair at all." He grinned at her. "Let's take turns. You ask a question in the first seminar, I'll do duty in the second one. That way they won't hate us right away."

"Perfect." Marian grinned. "So what led you here, anyhow?"

Albert stretched his arms up and out in a cat yawn. "My old man, down in Shelburne, saved all his life for one of his kids to do the minister thing. He's old school Anglican—one son for the church and such. Anyway, my brothers all got out before he could stick it on them. My oldest brother John got a lobster tag—hundred thou a year. Nobody in their right mind would let him turn that down. Big bro Bill joined the navy. He's never home. My near brother, Thom, took off to Alberta to work, without even asking. Which left me." He shrugged. "My dad hopes I'll do it. He always wanted to be a minister himself but he only had a grade five education. Barely able to read the Bible."

"I'll bet he knew a lot despite that," Marian said. "School isn't everything. The minister down our way was a PhD and useless." She touched Albert's arm, noticed its warmth. "Real life knowledge is often better."

"Yeah, probably. Didn't open any doors for him, though." He shrugged. "So, what draws you here, 'Miss Questions'?"

"Long story."

"Let's get an espresso. I want to hear it, but I'm thirsty."

They wandered across the St. Mary's campus in search of a cafe, talking and laughing as if they'd been friends forever. For the first time that day, Marian felt as if she might have made the right choice.

As they walked, they noticed rainbow signs encircling them. They hung everywhere to show solidarity with a LGBTQ community leader who'd been beaten and killed the previous month. Marian couldn't help shuddering. She'd seen far too much of lives being destroyed for being different—mentally ill or sexually divergent people in particular.

Marian and Albert argued about the case. The murderer was a local guy with violent mental health issues, and he'd been let out without supervision. Was it truly an assault on a gay man, or merely a confused attack by someone who didn't realize who they were attacking? Was it another example of the poor getting inadequate care from the system?

"They should lock that guy up and throw away the key. Mental illness isn't an excuse for murder," Albert growled.

Marian wasn't so sure she agreed. Couldn't the fellow need care more than punishment? She scowled at Albert, wondering if he was really a nice guy, or a conservative cloaked in politeness? She'd met a few of those over the years and they gave her hives.

Despite their argument, they both ended up signing a student petition to create a park in the victim's memory. It seems they saw some things the same, after all.

"Now, where's that damn Timmie's?" Albert spun to look.

The neighbourhood was sorely lacking in the usual Tim Horton's franchises. They eventually found a diner of sorts, its windows steamed up and menus in Chinese posted on the door. The door rattled as they went in, and they could feel the gale blowing through the edges. Always the wind.

Once they sat down and held hot brew in mugs that looked older than both of them, Albert leaned toward Marian. "So give," he said. "What brings a sceptic like you to la la land?"

"I got a scholarship?"

"Not enough."

Marian turned her cup back and forth, around and around.

"First, well, you realize I'm one of those 'mature student' types."

"Ooh," said Albert. "An older woman!"

"And you're how old?"

"Thirty."

"Ah. I'm not that much older. I'm thirty-three." Marian tapped him on the arm as punishment. Her finger bounced. Albert didn't seem thirty. He was still all supple and smooth and muscled. Marian instantly felt as dusty as a withered grandmother. It was a good thing there were several actual withered grandmothers in their group or she'd have crumpled into dust right then. "The other thing is, I'm married. Was married… to a military guy. Loved to order people around. They posted us everywhere—no kids, see—and he was deployed a lot. That's probably why we got along for as long as we did."

"And now? Is he here? Are you separated? Divorced?"

Marian shook her head. "He came home wrong after his time in Afghanistan. He got PTSD—so many do. Scary as hell. He lost it over there when the Afghans started shooting the Canadians sent to train them. He couldn't understand how he'd worked so hard to build their trust, only to have them turn it around and try to kill him. So he started returning fire. The Army shipped him back, dishonourable discharge, and it broke him." She sighed. "He decided to break me. I had to run away."

"Wow! Did he hurt you?"

"Not physically. It was only a matter of time, I'm sure. He was smashing things in the kitchen, destroyed our computer, things like that. His mother moved in with us and helped by stirring the pot."

"Horrible. Must have been scary to make yourself up and leave though—were you working there too, so you'd have to leave your job? How did you get away without him coming after you?"

"Yeah, my job." Marian gulped the last of her coffee and swiped her tongue over her teeth to dig at the grounds. "I sensibly did an English degree. Ended up working as a secretary for an insurance company, checking on insurance claims, putting up barriers to avoid paying out. Soul-destroying. As was the marriage. So I snuck away from them both. Neither knows where I am." She grinned, but it fell into a frown. "I suspect I have lost my chance at the 'employee of the year' prize."

Albert took a sip of his coffee, letting Marian gather her thoughts. "So you're here to find your destroyed soul?"

"I guess. My dad died and left me some money and I grabbed the earliest scholarship I could that let me escape New Brunswick. I knew I needed to be near the sea. And I do have an interest in theology…" Marian turned her coffee mug around in circles. "I sent Neil a letter once I was safely away. He still doesn't realize where I am and I'm not telling him. Yet."

"How long were you married?"

"Seven years. Last six months we spent in counseling. It

didn't take."

"Lots of time to know what your life would have been like if you stayed with him. Good for you to be brave enough to escape. Do the police have a restraining order on him or anything?"

Marian snorted. "Yeah, like those work. I don't want to do anything that lets him know where I am until he cools down. I have my friendly spies in Moncton who know guys who know him. I plan to check in with them every once in a while. I hear he's not cool yet."

Albert waved at the waitress. She came over and topped up their coffees, pulling two lukewarm creams out of her apron and throwing them on the table.

Albert peeled a top of one off and slurped out the contents, laughing at Marian's expression. "I used to do this when I was a kid. Seems appropriate. I'm feeling all childish and contrary." Marian smiled. "I don't really remember being a child." Albert made a poor you face. "Well, we've got to fix that! Have you ever been to glow-in-the-dark mini-golfing?"

"What? Never."

"Okay, it's a date, then. Next weekend?"

"You're on," Marian said, laughing. "What parts glow?"

"My secret. What's the time? Oh dammit. It's only twenty minutes until class and miles to go. Let's run."

3

Where it Began

The week passed, with Marian spending far too much time exploring Halifax with Albert, and far too little time studying. They laughed together as they strolled the new harbour boardwalk and photographed the drunken lamp poles, chased squirrels in Point Pleasant Park, hung out at The Old Triangle and Darrell's Restaurant, shared their new city. They ended up getting a season's pass at the glow in the dark golf place and even talked some of their less serious classmates into joining them. The fall ocean air seemed full of promise as it blew them around. They all enjoyed slipping away from the seriousness at AST and spending time simply laughing and looking.

It was nice to have easy conversations, too. The readings were definitely not easy. Marian struggled as she studied, trying to avoid flashbacks to the past, but every discussion of beliefs and the life of Yeshua and the early church brought them into her thoughts, loud and hurtful and bright.

Finally she shook herself and gave in, allowing herself an hour to straighten out her head. She made herself a cup of cocoa, set the oven timer, sat in the only vaguely comfortable chair in her student common room, and sent her thoughts back.

* * *

She could remember how everything started as clearly as a if she was watching a movie. She had been Miryam then. One day, she was up in the hills around Nazareth messing about with the lambs, despite her father warning her to stay close to home. The Romans were everywhere, tax-collecting and looting. But it was quiet up in the hills, and Miryam could escape the endless discussion of her betrothal and all that she needed to learn to be a bride and a stepmother to Yoseph-ben-Yacob's children. She would be the lead woman of her own household. It terrified her. She was only twelve, younger than some of Yoseph's daughters.

She'd met Yoseph, of course. He'd been hanging around for the last few years since his wife died, waiting for Miryam to grow up enough to wed. He seemed nice enough, if quiet, clumsy, and so very old. He was a builder with stone, not a carpenter like the other men—there weren't many trees to speak of where they lived, and they couldn't go to waste. Given Yoseph's tendency to drop everything whenever Miryam walked by, she wasn't too impressed with his skill. No wonder he'd had to take a poor wife.

They'd never spoken to each other directly. It wasn't allowed. Ever. Unmarried women, young or old, had to be careful about speaking to men. If they spoke to men, the village would stone them to a pulp. The men who spoke to the women didn't get rocks thrown at them, but they had to answer to the rabbi. It was yichud, forbidden, to even be in the same room with a man without chaperones. And if the door was shut? Terrible, terrible.

Miryam was only allowed to speak a word or two to Yoseph at her parents' table, when they were carefully supervised. Yoseph said what he wanted, whenever he wanted, for as long as he wanted. So many words. Miryam chewed and tried not to dread the endless nights ahead. Would he talk to her in those long angry sentences? Would he complain to her about money, taxes, rent? Make her eat his favourite fava beans?

Once, in the market, she watched a newly married couple. They were inside their stall and thought no one would see them, but Miryam spotted them through an opening in the curtains. They kissed one another, touched each other all over. Miryam wondered if she'd enjoy being touched in that way. She didn't think she would with Yoseph. His hands were already age-withered.

* * *

Now, several reincarnations later, Marian knew how sex felt. How it could feel warm and wonderful, tantalizing and tempting. Or cold and business-like, brutal and hurting. She'd been lucky enough to experience lust once or twice, that intoxicating tingling running up from the base of her spine. She'd also been unlucky enough to experience rape, in war and in marriage. Spent years alone or in cold marriages where the wall between spouses was too hard to melt with a touch.

4

Octavius

Back then, Miryam was an innocent, enjoying the curls of the soft lamb fleece, the warmth of the spring sun. So she was unprepared for the approach of a Roman Centurion. He galloped up beside her as she sat on the grass, a lamb dozing in her lap.

"What a lovely vision," he said, as he dismounted. He squatted beside her on the grass and stroked the lamb. She froze in fear, but he spoke to her in Aramaic, her own tongue, and, after looking around to be sure no one could see her, she gradually relaxed.

"What's your lamb's name?"

"We don't name them. I just call him Daniel."

"Why Daniel?"

Miryam pushed her fingers into the lamb's soft fleece. "It's a boy in my village…"

The Centurion laughed. "I'll bet you wish you were stroking the other Daniel like you are this lamb."

Miryam blushed and turned her head away.

"I'm sorry," he said. He put a finger under her chin and turned her face toward him. The heat of his finger was warmer than even the sunshine. "You're too young to jest about boys, aren't you? Still just a child."

"I'm twelve!" Miryam said. She hated being teased about being immature. It happened all the time. She was short and looked young for her age, skin sun-kissed a light brown, eyes wide and dark. "Besides, I'm already betrothed."

The Centurion sat back on his heels, whistling softly through his teeth. "Are they marrying you off to one of those horrible old men who have bred their first wives to death?"

"Yes," said Miryam, then realized what she'd said. "I mean, he's not horrible, but he is old. And his wife died."

The soldier swore under his breath. "And so, sweet lamb girl, soon he will take you in his bed and you'll only ever experience the love of a soft old man." He sighed, took a strand of her hair in his fingers and admired it. "It's a pity. And then you will be bred, and bred, until your hair goes all dry and flat."

Miryam stood up. Something was wrong. The intensity in the Centurion's eyes made her go wobbly inside.

"No, please don't go," the soldier said. "Sit with me and we won't talk about that any longer. See, I have some bread and cheese and figs and wine. Won't you share them with me?"

Miryam looked at his food bundles and her stomach betrayed her, calling out her hunger. Food was scarce at home since the last time the Romans had passed and burned their farms. The soldier held out his hand, filled with scraps of food. "I'm Octavius. What may I call you?"

"Miryam," she mumbled. She reached for his hand and the food. And if his hand lingered a moment on hers, surely it was only to keep the bread from falling?

"The sun is hot here," said Octavius. "Let's sit in the shade over there. My horse would be glad of the respite."

They stood and walked over to a large boulder, a little way off the path. And if his hand laid in the small of her back as they walked, surely it was only to steady her on the stony ground? Miryam tilted as she walked, light-headed, uncertain how to deal with the pressure from his hand, with his resonant voice, with the unexpected feelings in her body.

They ate, almost silent, making comments now and then about the sheep or the clouds. The cheese, warm from the sun, ran down their fingers and onto the bread. It was delicious.

After it was all gone, Octavius tenderly pulled Miryam back against him. "Now you must relax, little one. Lean on me. The climb up here must have tired you."

Miryam knew she shouldn't, that she should leave, but he was so polite, so solid, and seemed so safe, almost fatherly. She laid against his chest as his arms closed about her and dozed. The walk up to the sheep had been long and dry after doing all her usual housework. When she relaxed, Octavius stroked her, as she'd stroked the lamb. He ran his hand down her hair again and again, absentminded, until Miryam became very sleepy. Then he stroked her arms, down to her fingers, rolling each one between his fingers. He lifted one of her hands to his mouth and sucked off the cheese still on her fingertips. Miryam tried to pull her hand back, but he held it there and the warmth in his mouth, the sensation of his tongue on her finger, the sharpness of his teeth transfixed her with contrasts. He licked her finger, making thrills run over her in waves. She had never experienced these sensations.

Curious, Miryam pulled his finger up to her mouth and tentatively licked it. He tasted salty, like his horse, like the cheese they'd been eating. Octavius moaned, pulled Miryam closer, kissed her hair. She felt languid and thrilled all at once, filled with unfamiliar sensations, unwilling to move away from them. Then he moved his hands lower, stroking her legs, pulling up her robe bit by bit. Realizing her danger at last, Miryam struggled in his arms, but he flipped her over and was on top of her. She writhed, tried to kick him, spat at his face. He laughed, pushed her hair away from her face and kissed her.

The sound of men yelling made him pull away, stand up, and rearrange his clothing. A crowd of angry shepherds arrived around the rocks, carrying sticks and shouting Miryam's name. Octavius moved back, put his hand on the hilt of his sword as it hung from his saddle. Miryam leapt to her feet and ran to the shepherds, weeping in fright, and not so much because of Octavius. Her family would be furious that she had spent time alone with a man—a Roman!

Judas, the leader of the group, shoved her back to the rear of the group where her kinsmen gathered. "What were you doing with our woman?" He turned to Miryam. "Are you well, Miryam? Because if not…"

Miryam nodded, still pulled into herself, ashamed of the feelings she'd let happen.

Octavius laughed, "If you don't want to lose your women, stop leaving them out like bait. Especially lovely ones like your sweet Miryam."

The group roared and rattled their sticks. Octavius sprung into his saddle. He pulled his sword partway out so it glinted in the sun. The men shuffled backwards. They'd seen what swords from on high could do.

"Please, let him go! He just shared his food with me. I am fine!" Miryam cried. They all stared at her, open-mouthed.

"It's true!"

"I'm on my way," Octavius said. "No harm done, just a little food shared. Enjoy your wedding, charming Miryam!" Octavius turned his horse and cantered down the path. He didn't turn around. For a moment, Miryam felt a strange pang of loss.

"What were you playing at?" Judas bellowed at Miryam. "Why were you alone—with a Roman? The scum that are bleeding us dry! Why did you let him speak to you? How did he know your name? Whore!"

Miryam cringed. "He spoke so gently. I didn't want to get him upset. He might have attacked me."

"He might have anyway! Are you still intact? How will we know?" Judas sneered. "Wee Daniel says you are 'special.' He tells me you aren't for purchase, not like the other women we find with the Romans. And yet here you are, selling yourself for some simple bread."

Miryam blushed to the roots of her scalp. "He didn't touch me, I tell you. He had some cheese and bread and wine. I was hungry, so I ate. He was just leaving when you came up." The lie was awkward, but needed. If she didn't hold to her story, they would examine her in many unpleasant and personal ways when she got back, and they would humiliate her in front of her father and Yoseph. "I am no fan of the Romans, you know that! We have had little food to spare since they have taken all our stores in tax and fire. Doesn't that entitle me to some of his rations?" She flung her hair back and put her hands on her hips. Maybe if she pretended to be the one in charge of the exchange, they would believe her. "That was more than any of you rebels have given me! Would you deny me food he took from us?"

Judas paused. "But you were alone with him nonetheless. This is forbidden. I don't imagine hearing of this will please your betrothed or your family."

Miryam shrunk again. "Must you tell them?" She spun around, showing her intact clothing. "See! Nothing happened."

"Yes, but you are late back to the village and they all are aware we set out after you. They all saw a Centurion heading this way. How else will we explain your delay?"

Miryam thought quickly, scrutinizing the crew. They looked a mess. "You are living in the hills, I hear. Without food or water."

Judas nodded. "It is our safe place. They are already looking for us. We have to move from that place, too, now that a Roman knows where we are." He turned to his men, who made themselves busy rearranging their makeshift weapons and lifting their packs. They knew an order when they saw one.

"What if I brought you food and wine in exchange for your silence? I'm small and can slip away—no one cares about me— and I do a lot of the cooking. I can sneak some supplies up to you."

They muttered to each other. They were starving, thought Miryam.

"I'll even wash some of your clothing. I can put it in with the family's and they will never notice." The men scuffed their feet, watching Judas for guidance. In exasperation, she blurted, "I can even make you some new clothing, wouldn't that be nice?"

Judas looked at them, breathed in their filth. They were all dressed in rags after months hiding in the hills. He conceded. "Our silence for your help. We have a deal." He reached out and shook Miryam's arm, in a man's handshake. He turned to the men. "If any of you speak of this, I will hand you over in chains to the Romans. You, too, Miriam. Understood?"

One or two men nodded. Several of them gulped, and one scratched at a fleabite. New, less flea-ridden clothes must sound like a great idea, Miryam thought. She dipped her head in agreement, afraid to speak.

"We will tell everyone you fell asleep in the heat, yes? We came across you sleeping and woke you up." Judas looked to his men for their agreement. They nodded, slowly. "You'll be punished for taking such an irresponsible risk, Miryam, but no more."

She bent her head, and with that Miryam began her second service life.

* * *

Miryam brought wine and scraps of food to the ever-growing camp of rebel Judeans. Often she had to pretend to go to bed and sneak out at night to escape her house and the eyes of her mother and father. She was being practically guarded after being late back, almost as if they didn't believe she had fallen asleep. Her father had struck her with his cane when she got back, furious. Her mother was still terrified she would make foolish mistakes and cause Yoseph to cancel her betrothal. The family needed his money.

Her parents even tried to make the marriage happen sooner, but that would mean Yoseph and Miryam would wed before she was of age, which was bad luck. No one wanted that, especially Yoseph, who wanted more children. Boys. A bad luck marriage would endanger that. His dead wife might return to haunt them and make Miryam's womb barren. The rabbi warned against it and refused to finish the betrothal.

As Miryam stole back and forth to the hidden camp up in the mountains, she ended up talking to the men, often sitting with them while they ate to carry the empty vessels back. That way she could return the pots to the kitchen before anyone noticed their absence, she rationalized. Plus, it was taboo, so it had an extra thrill about it. She was still a child. Disobedience was forever a temptation, no matter how much she tried to be the dutiful daughter.

She'd mend their clothing by the fire, too, or sew things for them. As she spoke with the group, she found her affection for Daniel growing. They already knew each other from when they were babies and had played together when they were small. Unlike the others in the camp, he would make her warm tea when she arrived and wrap her up in blankets against the cold. He told funny stories that made everyone laugh. Every time she brought them something, he'd make a point of thanking her, and she thrilled to the sound of his voice.

They started off sitting beside each other, then Daniel offered to walk her partway home in the dark. Soon they were stealing touches as they walked away from the fire. Touches grew into hugs, hugs into kisses, kisses into even greater contact. Over the months, they explored more of what the Centurion had started.

"I can't do what you want," she protested to Daniel. She knew more about sex now as her aunt Sarah had taken her along to birthings, getting her ready for her own. "The rabbi forbids. Moses forbade! I'm betrothed. I am already claimed. You can't touch me there!" She said no in so many ways she was sure he would hear her.

Daniel shook his head in frustration. "Isn't all skin the same?"

he asked. Then he offered to marry her. She refused. "But you love me!" he cried. "You don't have to marry old Yoseph! You could join us and help us fight the Romans."

It tempted Miryam, but she also knew her parents depended on her marriage, on the support of Yoseph and his family. So she brought them food and clothing and herself and returned home, intact.

She couldn't stop seeing him, though. The Judeans needed her support, and Daniel's soft laugh made Miryam melt. She started to want to touch him more, to give him pleasure as he did her. They held off for months, tension building, until the Judean crowd brought in a rebel rabbi to marry them. They couldn't stand Daniel's moodiness anymore.

The rabbi blessed their union, while admitting he could no longer technically do so. The Temple had fired him for his political statements, afraid of Roman repercussions. Instead, he kept hidden with the rebels and prayed with them. In the ceremony, Miryam vowed to never be a full wife to Yoseph, and to seek her freedom as soon as possible. It was the only available compromise.

The rebel Judeans had a very quiet but happy celebration, and Daniel and Miryam fell into each other's arms in joy. The crowd of men had set up a marriage tent for them, and Daniel pulled her in behind him, quickly, to the laughs of the rest of the camp.

Once Miryam made love with Daniel, she felt they should do it more often. Daniel agreed. And so they did. And did. It was part of a good marriage according to the Torah, they told each other. Not that they needed much convincing.

In-between, the Judeans planned their attacks, bolstered by Miryam's good food. They became stronger, healthier. More ready to take risks. For Miryam, it was an exciting existence, filled with thrills, romance, and a sense of importance.

Until the day a great wailing from the village awakened her.

5

Slaughter and Surprise

"Whatever is happening?" cried Miryam's mother. No one answered her, the wailing too loud for her voice to carry. "Go find out, Miryam!"

Miryam pulled on a covering and pushed her way through to the centre of the throng. Their rabbi was standing on a little table to be certain they could see him and waving his arms. "Silence, silence!" he called. "Do not create so much noise!" His urgent tone hushed the crowd. He dropped his arms and spoke. "The soldiers might hear us. We must pretend all is well, or they will visit the same disaster on our town. They know where many of the boys came from."

There was an in-drawing of breath like a dry desert wind.

"Disaster?" Miryam said to herself, wondering.

"Yes," responded her cousin Rachel, who had arrived beside her. "Those Judeans have gone too far this time."

"No. Oh no! What did they do?"

"They broke into the tax building and set fire to all the tax registers. Now the Romans can't extract any more money until they have renewed their records—no one knows who owes what. The collectors were furious."

A man in the crowd started laughing and weeping and clutching his wife to him. "No taxes! We're saved!" Other villagers were dancing and cheering. Miryam stared at them.

"Yes," said Rachel. "He will have his farm back now there is no record of his debts. All of us have a new start, for a while."

"Are they all gone?" Miryam asked. She was thinking of her parents' taxes. Could she get out of her betrothal if they were debt-free? She could marry Daniel in public after all!

"Yes, the whole group. Gathered them up and sent them off to crucify, the soldiers did."

"The debts?" Miryam asked, confused.

"No, stupid, the Judeans. The cabal you've been feeding up on the hillsides. The guard surrounded them. They weren't able fight them all."

"You saw?"

"Of course I noticed. You can't pull the wool over my eyes. One mother had a son in the group and informed me about your tricks, but I didn't betray you. Yoseph and your parents don't know. Praise Jehovah you weren't there when the Romans came!"

Miryam sat, hard, on a rock in the yard. All gone? All of them? Judas, the fearless leader? Her Daniel? "Are they all being crucified?" Her hands shook.

"They already were, this morning. All your effort, for nothing. Maybe you'll settle down now. It's time to grow up." Rachel swept away, dragging her scorn like a train behind her.

Miryam folded into a ball, weeping, weeping. The other families wept, too, quieter than before, and then filtered off to their homes to grieve in private. Miryam had no family with whom to share her grief when she crept home, so she explained to her mother what had taken place and fell into bed.

She lay down and cried, and lay and cried for a whole week, until her mother lost patience with her. "Grow up, get out! It's not like any of our people died! You must support the others."

So Miryam did. In the sorrow of that time, she lost track of the days, and so it was very late on that she recognized that she was carrying Daniel's baby.

* * *

At first, she didn't panic. Miryam studied with the midwives in their village and knew of the herbs they used to prevent and end a pregnancy. Miryam decided she would ask her aunt Sarah, the midwife she worked most with, about dosage and sources. About how to simulate virginity when it had been surrendered. And, thought Miryam with a sigh, if Yoseph found out and chose not to wed her, even if she appeared again virgin, she could always become a midwife herself. It was a regular and respectable occupation for unmarried women. Perhaps that would help offset her family's financial loss.

She relaxed. That's what she'd do. She'd already helped deliver her friend Ruth's second baby and showed she had the touch. Poor Ruth! They married her to a brutal husband. They wed when she was twelve and he was seventy, and it was obvious he planned to breed her to death. She'd previously had two children, both girls. After the second baby in two years, Ruth had started her endless weeping. Only a boy would give her any rest.

Maybe there were worse situations than being unmarried, Miryam decided.

She wanted her baby with one part of her, blushed with shame with another. If the village discovered she was pregnant, they might beat her, stone her, send her out to live alone in the hills, even punish her family. The prospect terrified her.

As they were helping with a birth in the village, Miryam whispered to Sarah about the medicine to interrupt a pregnancy, pretending it was for a local girl. Sarah slipped her a tiny bundle pulled from the drying herbs she had hanging on her wall, warning her to not mention them to anyone. Miryam made a tincture of them, boiling the herbs in a kettle late at night and gulping down the bitter liquid. She was so hoping they'd remove the little bud inside her and save her, but soon enough she realized the pregnancy wasn't going anywhere.

She had to confess her situation to someone, make a plan, sort out how the both of them could live. She knew she shouldn't mention Daniel to anyone, sure the Romans would come back and kill his child. The Roman soldiers acted on grudges in monstrous ways, and they were still traveling about wreaking havoc in return for the Judean attack. They had already slaughtered an entire village's sons and animals for no reason except that a farmer mentioned taxes in their hearing. So, trembling, she sought Sarah and made up a story about Octavius, making the date of his attack more recent, watching the shock creep across her aunt's face.

"But… a Roman? A Centurion? One of those vermin that burned our village? That killed our boys?"

Miryam nodded, let a tear fall out of her eye. The tears were real. She missed Daniel, wished they could have run away and had their own little family.

Sarah was still ranting, brandishing her arms. "It was rape. I should report him! Not that they'll do anything, but maybe you can get something for the baby. What was his name?"

"I don't remember," said Miryam. "He never said." Another serious lie, and she didn't know why she said it. The chances of meeting Octavius again were slight. She wouldn't bring him back into the story; lying was bad enough when it only involved her.

"What will you tell your parents? And Yoseph? Aiee—this is terrible! He'll never marry you now. What shall we do?"

They tried more herbs for abortion, but though Miryam was ill for five full days, causing her mother to watch her every mouthful of food, the pregnancy stayed rooted. She finally understood she had no choice but to tell her parents.

She picked an evening when Yoseph was at her home for dinner, and only her parents, Yoseph and Miryam were eating together. It did not go well. Yoseph stormed about and spat at her. Her mother wept; her father negotiated. They increased her dowry. Yosef relented when the price was high enough.

He made a huge sulky fuss, and he told everyone in his family that he wasn't the father of Miryam's baby, shaming her before them. But he needed a woman to look after his household and children, and he couldn't be too choosy. He was old and poor and his children were hellions. The sons were loud and large and given to excesses of everything. And the daughters were vicious! Miryam fell into bed exhausted every night, especially as pregnancy made her belly huge.

Yoseph eventually demanded his marriage rights, averting his face as he thrust. Miryam soon found out that Octavius had been right. Loving an old man differed greatly from loving a young one.

6

Reincarnation

Marian stretched her neck back and forth, coming rapidly forward to the present. Her cocoa was cold. There wasn't much point in revisiting these memories, she told herself angrily. Unless there was some lesson she'd missed, and that's why she was coming back and back again. She had met no one else who seemed to reincarnate, recycle the way she did.

The stacking up lives were so discouraging. She longed for rest. It was demoralizing, constantly returning with barely a break between generations. She was tired of pretending not to be an ancient soul in a youthful frame. She was so fed up with living in a body through all the changes of life—babyhood, adolescence, giving birth, aging. Death. Then going through it all again. And always as a woman. If she'd had a chance to be a man once or twice, it might have at least been amusing. How many times would she have to come back? How much longer? Hadn't she paid enough? What was she meant to learn?

Frustrated, she threw on a sweater and went for a walk along the waterfront, watching the boats bob up and down at the yacht club. The wind was blowing fresh, and it helped her clear her thoughts. She even tried praying to the Triune God, as her professor kept referring to him. Maybe that Lord would listen better than her Old Testament one. That God seemed to have shunned her for her behaviour before Yeshua was born. The Father that Yeshua had spoken of appeared to be a more tolerant sort, although she wasn't sure of that now, tired as she was. She did know she wasn't forgiven.

* * *

The first rebirth had been exciting, she remembered. It took her a while to get her feet under her, understand that it was her, though in a new skin. It came to her once she reached her teens. One day she realized that she already knew things—midwifery, caring for the ill, cooking and washing and even shreds of a different language. It terrified her for several months until the visions grew clear and she settled into her new body. She was taller this time and had green eyes she couldn't help staring at in the glass. Men stared at them, too. Her family lived on a coast, and her father and brothers were fishermen on the ocean. They ate well and grew hearty.

Then named Mary, she went to her rabbi for confession. A lot. She could never bring herself to discuss that first deception about Daniel and Octavius, but her guilt was heavy. She asked herself again and again if she was the cause of Daniel's death— her God was fond of smiting in vengeance. But then, why had she survived? It made little sense and was confusing during this reincarnation.

As she reincarnated again and again she, bewildered, watched the vision of her son creep across Europe, their religion infiltrate the world, and their message of peace repeat and be translated and twisted. Wars blew through, too, and plagues. Religions waxed during times of trial, she noted. Everyone needed reassurance from an all-powerful deity.

Then she was created in a 'Christian' family, which was unsettling. Her head spun. Who was she then? Who was she worshipping? She could barely keep track of herself.

That was a wild, murderous time. Even the newly forming convents weren't safe—they pulled out the more tempting sisters and raped or martyred them if they fought the assaults. Most of the townswomen had already sickened or died in childbirth or of some dread illness, and many of the nuns were healthy, young, and desirable, with their own teeth and untouched skin. Then, as in many other times, it wasn't safe to be a young woman, especially an attractive one.

In this life, Mary did the only thing she could think of—hid herself in the local convent's kitchen, let her hair fall over her face and never bathed. She smelled atrociously of fire and rotting meat and her head was full of lice, and the men never even glanced her way. If she had known she would live as long as she did that lifetime, she would have washed, suffered the men's attacks and died. As it was, she grew old and toothless and pain-weary. Staggering on damaged hips, she spilled a pot of broth on her foot and burned it. It went gangrenous; the pain was excruciating as it spread. She eventually took some herbs she'd studied in a previous generation and shortened her life herself.

7

Where it Ended

Marian tugged the hair back off of her face—those ocean winds were making her usually straight hair explode in the humidity—and wandered back to the calm residence, thoughts frothing like the waves. Maybe that second sin, euthanasia, was the reason for her endless reincarnations? She'd helped others end their lives, but only when she saw all hope was gone. But would any God want her or others to be so wretched, to rot away on their bones? What was the point? She never understood the need for the end-of-life pain. But she'd been wrong before, she knew. She learned over the generations that martyrdom often required pain—burning, beating, even cutting off of breasts. Maybe even life alone required suffering.

Marian, exhausted by her thoughts, crawled into bed, pulling the gnostic gospels in with her. She hadn't read James in her past lives—it wasn't on the list of commonly read biblical treatises. The Old Testament was the God she was most familiar with from her lives before, many of them in Jewish families. She was so far behind her fellow students. She needed to read the birth story in James before she fell asleep.

A half hour later, she was up and pacing the floor, knotting her fists. Rage twisted her face. How could they have gotten it so wrong? Hadn't they listened to her at all?

* * *

Marian recalled the faces of the apostles after they'd buried Yeshua. Then, too late, they wanted to hear everything about him. After all the weeks she spent following them about, cooking for them, cleaning for them, finding them places to stay, they finally realized she might have something meaningful to say about her own son's life. Then, they sat around her like puppies, asking questions over and over, making sure they had it all down right. She was so patient, controlled her anger. Smiled when she would have preferred to box their ears for being so dense. And after all that, what she told them had been transcribed into something like this? Marian was seething.

Miryam and the other women had worked like slaves. Following Yeshua was like an endless camping trip, always on the move, scraping food from leavings, repairing clothes and shoes. Never sleeping on comfortable bed. And Mary Magdalene—Magda? She was no use. She trotted after Yeshua like a little lamb, adoring his every movement. Even after they married, she didn't do her full share of chores, but at least then Miryam could rope her into helping with laundry days now and then. She tried not to mind. Every mother wants a woman for their son that adores them, and Magda most assuredly did that.

* * *

Absolutely none of this was in the book Marian was reading. It was all angels this and Holy Spirit that. Marian smiled a little at Daniel being given that title. It would have appealed to his urge for glory.

According to this tripe, she was somehow impregnated after talking to an angel, no contact involved. Where was the fun for her in that? And poor old Yoseph was apparently told by an angel he had to marry her. What was with all these angels flying around the place? Marian had never seen a single winged human shaped thing, not in 2000 years. Not even a ghostly shape of one.

The Gospel didn't credit Miryam's role as the mother to Yoseph's many children, their children, but they were sure to mention many, many times that Yoseph wasn't the father of Miryam's first child, so apparently she was to carry that shame forever. Fortunately, they seemed not to know about Daniel, which allowed her to keep him to herself, her guilty secret love.

In fact, they'd written Miryam out of the story, thought Marian, gritting her teeth until the back one hurt. After all those hours she spent looking after them before and after Yeshua died, telling them stories of his childhood, how she taught him and saw to his upbringing, how she encouraged him to be kind to women, all of that was gone. Lost, forgotten.

The other gospels also damned Magda, she learned, described her as a whore or possessed. Her son would have had a few words to say about that!

It was as if they hated anyone but them having a relationship with Yeshua. Marian threw her book down, picked it up, threw it again. She sat on the edge of her bed and sobbed. In all of her lives, she had never felt so degraded, negated, and abandoned. That said a lot, all these experiences later. What did it all mean?

Was she here to teach her humility? Was this part of the Plan? The ineffable Plan?

Still angry, she stuffed the book under her pillow and tried to doze off. She turned on CBC Radio to distract herself and finally fell asleep listening to their overnight broadcasting. Tonight's included a section from Wales on how to make cheese. It was oddly reassuring.

8

The Women

The next day was Marian's first day at the Compass program. She smiled as she walked down the stairs at King's United Church, hearing laughter bubbling up from the basement. Young mothers and pregnant girls filled the room, giggling with excitement about their babies and toddlers. They pushed broken down strollers and wore clothes from the local thrift shop, no doubt. But there was joy here. And love. This place would suit her perfectly. Dr. Rutgers had chosen well for her.

Marian sought the only other member of the group without a tattoo, a diminutive, gentle-faced blonde woman named Nancy. She was the leader, a psychologist, but she'd taken care to dress for the crowd in a sweatshirt and jeans. Marian liked her instantly. Nancy's smile reached all the way to her eyes.

"Oh, I'm so glad to see you!" Nancy greeted her. She hugged her, and Marian, startled, hugged her back. "Dr. Rutgers told me you were just the person I needed. You know about parenting, right?"

Marian grinned. "Oh yes, I know a little." She had parented

many, many, many years over. Her grandchildren were legion. She might even be related to Nancy, or any of the mothers here.

"Perfect," said Nancy, "these women—they've all somehow lost their family support, if there was any to start with. They're all so young, but they've already been in trouble. They just need to build their self-confidence and get some connections and survival skills to change their lives around. And they need food. Good food for them and their babies."

Marian looked around her. There were more tattoos and needle-tracks and piercings in that room than she'd seen in her life before. Some of them looked tougher than the wives she potato-farmed with in her time in Bosnia in the 20s. And that was saying something.

Nancy peered up at her. "You are okay with this, right?"

Marian nodded and smiled. How could she say no, when she'd been in this position so many times herself, dependent on the help of strangers?

"One more thing," said Nancy, her voice rising, "you're for sure not going to pray over them or demand we say grace, or anything, are you? It would turn them right off."

"It's extremely unlikely," Marian said.

"Good. The last student had a horrible time. I might not tell them where you are from right away. Well, grab a seat in the circle and I'll introduce you. We usually have a chat first and then a few of us prepare something to snack on and we share it. Everyone has a duty—making the meal or cleaning up or packing the bags of food. We send everyone home with some things we've cooked and a bag of other stuff from the food bank. It's why they come, but they make friends here, too, and that helps."

She added, "Sometimes we have guest speakers. I could sure use some help to round people up. My ideas are all boring by now."

"What do they like to talk about?"

"We'll ask them again today," Nancy said. "It's their choice but often they can't think of anyone, so it helps to have some ideas to pitch."

Marian liked the sound of the group already. Led by the women themselves and giving that vital support of others— she needed it so often. And when it was missing, things were so terribly lonely.

The Compass group seemed joyous despite the challenges the women endured. They all brought clothes to trade, complimented each other, laughed, offered man and sleep and shopping advice as they jiggled their babies. Nancy was present but not obtrusive. The women trusted Nancy, and Marian hoped they would come to count on her, too. Each week, she helped cook the 'snack,' really a full meal. She ladled soups and leftovers into stained margarine containers and the scratched old Tupperware that they found in a thrift store. She sang songs to the babies and held them and tried not to give advice she had gathered from many places and the past two thousand years. Though it was hard not to share what she had learned, she didn't want to appear too experienced. People might ask questions she couldn't answer without sounding dangerously strange.

* * *

Marian knew she had been born and died many times. Lives she barely remembered. She tried to add them up once and figured at least twenty-five so far—but she realized she forgot quite a few. One life she recalled only faintly, where she was placed without clothing or water on a mountainside, an unwanted female infant. Not uncommon then. She remembered nothing but the cold and the thousands of stars above. And the howling of wolves, singing to the moon.

There were other voids in her memory. Perhaps her life ended before she fully inhabited it, and someone returned her to wait for the next incarnation.

It confused Marian that she kept coming back as a healer, a woman named some variant of Mary. Each time she reincarnated, she felt the fabric of her soul grow thinner. She read about Nirvana and wondered if this was all about getting there. Was she moving closer, or farther away? What would it feel like if she got there?

She only ever met two people in all her lives who mentioned their reincarnation. They were Buddhist monks and assumed they were here to show others the path to paradise. Unlike them, Marian figured her recycling stemmed from something she'd forgotten to do. Some responsibility. Something left unconnected. Or possibly she wasn't acceptable yet?

Sometimes Marian tried to get through an entire reincarnation without thinking about her former one. It was difficult, especially when she would hunt for the proper word in one language and come out with one in another, ancient tongue. She would end up being slammed back into her memories, much like now with her studies at AST. Marian hoped this time at the school was meant to figure herself out, and when she did, she could rest.

9

Birthday

The women reminded her of those early few weeks at Yoseph's house. Yoseph rarely touched her, avoided her. He turned his whole body away when she walked past. The women in his household acted differently. They welcomed her into the full family, filled with sisters, brothers, children, babies, concubines, and cousins. For a poor builder, Yoseph supported a sizable group of people. The others were glad of some help.

She was lucky to have all the experienced mothers around to support her through her pregnancy. Though she'd studied with the midwives, it was a completely different thing experiencing it herself. She worried about everything, couldn't eat. She was so lonely and heartbroken for Daniel. The women made her special treats of figs, poured her wine, coaxed her to take one more bite.

For some reason, Yoseph dragged her all over the place the weeks before she delivered. He said he didn't want to leave her and had to do business visits, right then and requiring her company. She couldn't help wondering if he was trying to get her to lose the babe, though he seemed not to care enough to wish that upon her. It would have slowed their travels. He even organized a donkey for her to ride when she'd been too tired to walk. She wasn't sure if he cared or was just making sure they kept up the pace.

When her waters broke, far from home, Yoseph transformed from the cold husband she knew to a surprisingly tender one. It was almost as if someone had taken him aside and told him to shape up. He spent actual money for a place for her to rest, unglamorous shed though it was, and hired some women to assist her. He brought her drinks and food as she laboured.

She appreciated his unexpected kindness. Miryam's labour went on for hours, and if she hadn't attended so many other births, she might have given up. It wasn't a particularly painful birth, but it took forever. She was still only thirteen and not big in the hips. She struggled and heaved until the local midwife, heaving a sigh of relief, pulled out a huge baby boy.

Exhausted, Miryam lay back, watching the other women fuss over her baby—Daniel's child. She felt sobs gather in her throat at the memory of Daniel, but the midwives assumed they were tears of joy.

"Don't cry. You have a lovely son," said one, patting her hand. "Blessings on you, Miryam. A fine boy for Yoseph. Why he looks just like him!"

Miryam cringed. Babies look much the same, right? Would Yoseph hate the boy on sight, knowing he was not the father? Surely he couldn't shun such a handsome child. She couldn't stop looking at her son. He was beautiful, almost glowing. The boy was large, well rounded, with lighter skin than his mother, sturdy limbs, and eyes that seemed to see far into the distance.

Yoseph strode into the shed, pulled back the wrap from the

infant, and stood stock still. Miryam, afraid, huddled under the blankets. Surely he would beat her now, now that the birth was done. Instead, weeping, he lifted the child out of Miryam's arms, and crowed in joy. "A glorious boy!" he said. "Truly a gift from God." Yoseph leaned forward and touched Miryam's hair gently. "And you are an amazing mother. Look at the size of him!"

"What will be his name?" one midwife whispered to Miryam.

"No, no, not until naming day." Yoseph waved a finger at the curious midwives. "Let's see how he does."

Miryam trembled with fear. Their people did not name children until they passed the delicate first few days. Was Yoseph just pretending to be fond of her son until he could get rid of him? She looked at Yoseph, kissing and cuddling the babe. Or could he truly care for him?

The midwives clucked in disapproval, but Yoseph held the boy the entire time that they delivered the placenta and washed Miryam. For the seven days she rested after the birth, and whenever she wasn't feeding the baby, Yoseph was carrying him around, holding him tight, as if he was his own son. He showed him off to passing strangers, pointing out his clear eyes, his toes, the roundness of his belly. Then he would laugh delightedly and cuddle the baby again. Everyone stared at them.

When the midwives checked Miryam, they were astonished that she hadn't torn during the delivery. The baby had such a huge head, and his mother was so small! But no, she was intact, unhurt. Her cervix re-closed as tightly as a virgin's.

Yoseph's extreme interest in the child was unusual enough that the midwives were all gossiping about it. When they chattered back to their village, everyone clamoured to see this unusual family of an old man, a child bride, and a glowing son. They ended up with a lot of visitors those first days.

It was exhausting, but how could she turn away people who asked to look at her sweet baby and caring husband? They often brought food, too, and Miryam wanted to eat. As did her son. He nursed all the time. One awful family from the village down the hill dragged their child, and his noisy play drum, right in to beside the makeshift cradle. The baby had just fallen asleep, but the drummer played and played until he woke up and grimaced, ready to cry. "He smiled at me, he smiled at me," he yelled at his parents, who finally had the good grace to haul him away.

Somehow the local shepherds heard about the boy and within days the baaing and shuffling of sheep filled the door of the shed. Worried about the noise and smell, Yoseph pushed them all outside, humans and sheep, but the shepherds lingered until he took the wee one out to show him off. They gazed at their son and seemed overwhelmed.

Miryam couldn't understand the fuss. Of course, she loved her baby, but it seemed like they were adoring him. She was glad when it was near naming day and they could start the trek homewards.

* * *

Just before they set out, a group of astronomers passed by the stable and demanded to see the baby and his parents. It was practically the last straw for Miryam, whose hospitality was sorely tested by all the villagers and shepherds. How exciting was a new baby and a loving father, anyway? Most of the visitors who visited barely spoke to Miryam, except to praise

46

her birthing prowess. She felt positively bovine. Annoyed at yet another interruption, she pulled her baby off her breast, tidied her robe and hair, and prepared herself to be charming. Fortunately, this time the men were all business.

"We have been traveling all over this area," one said, "and heard that King Herod is slaughtering baby boys. He speaks of a dream that his reign would be brought to an end by a boy born this year, and he's decided to end that challenge before it begins. Slip home the back way. Stay off the main roads. Hide your son as much as possible." The man handed Miryam several large wraps and backed away. "Leave soon," he added. "We hear his troops are headed this way. The comet isn't helping—it lights the way here."

Miryam and Yoseph looked at each other in panic. Yoseph quickly packed their few travel belongings onto a camel lent by one of the astronomers. Miryam sat up high on its lumpy back, clutching the tightly wrapped baby to her chest. The rocking motion of the camel walking helped soothe him and the closeness of Miryam's breasts kept him fed. Still, it was a long and frightening trip home, keeping the baby quiet and hidden. The back roads were also favourites of bandits, so they had to travel by day, looking for a sign of oncoming soldiers every minute. It had been dry and hot, so any passers-by raised a spiral of dust. The wind blew it away in seconds.

When they finally arrived in their village, Yoseph's family exclaimed over the child, who they agreed to name Yeshua. They took care of Miryam until her purification date and spoiled Yeshua by carrying him everywhere. When word came to the house that the King still planned to kill all male Jewish babies, the women dressed Yeshua up as a girl, letting his hair grow long and giving him dollies to hold. They called him

Rebekah and never let him appear uncovered. They treated many of the other male children in the village the same, and if any wandering representative of the King came by, the people told them that the soldiers had already taken their sons, leaving only their daughters. It seemed to fool the soldiers, at least enough for them to leave. Miryam suspected they were not fond of their assignment and didn't look too closely.

When the King at last died and the killing of babies stopped, Yeshua and the other children were finally revealed as boys. They were still young enough to be happy in any clothing and made the change with no trouble. Miryam often wondered if those first few years as a daughter helped Yeshua understand and love women as he did.

10

Albert

Things had changed little in the clothing department, thought Marian. The women at the Compass program still dressed their babies in pink or blue, instantly sortable by gender. But if you changed the clothes, would the babies change their apparent sex? Probably. Babies rarely looked male or female, in Marian's experience.

Lisa, a gaunt sixteen-year-old carrying a huge baby dressed in navy blue coveralls sidled up to Marian. "Could you hold him? I've got to pee, and he's fussy."

Marian smiled at her. "I'd love to," she said. "He's a big guy, isn't he?"

"Twenty-five pounds," Lisa said, beaming. "He's only six months old. My boyfriend says I must have seal milk." She scurried to the bathroom, leaving Marian with a baby on the inhale, ready to scream.

"Now, now," said Marian, turning him to look away from her so he wouldn't make strange. She walked around the room, doing the age-old mother jiggle until he calmed down. She wanted to soothe him by stroking his forehead, as she'd done so often with her own babies, but she needed both hands just to carry him.

"You're good at that," Nancy said, coming up beside her.

"Lots of experience. Lots and lots." Marian realized what she'd said. "I mean, I worked at a daycare."

"I'll bet you'd be a good mum, too." Nancy touched her shoulder and left to join the women in the kitchen.

Marian paled and hoped that was the end of the mother talk. This life she did all she could to avoid having kids. She slipped up and got pregnant once, but with Neil becoming so angry, she was glad to have miscarried. Violent family dynamics were familiar to her. She'd felt the blows, seen the damage. Far better to ensure a child was wanted and loved. Also, after all these years, she was never sure if the man she took to her bed was a relative. It was getting muddled, all these reincarnations.

In her quiet moments, she wondered if she ever sent in one of those origin tests how her DNA would read. Maybe she'd be like that Newfoundland woman whose DNA showed up in every other Newfoundlander after her arrival on the island. Most likely, she'd freak out the laboratory technicians.

Looking around her, at all the happy women in the room, she felt a washing of sadness, a sudden feral regret she wouldn't ever have another baby of her own. Then she saw Nancy holding a screaming baby while hugging her teen mother and putting extra food in her take home bag. The sadness passed.

* * *

The next day, Marian and Albert met for coffee before seminar to talk about their placements. They fought their way through to the counter in the coffee shop in the Dalhousie Student

Union building and squashed into the far corner table. It was away from most of the spilled organic milk and the student babble.

"How was the drop-in?" Albert asked, stirring in his usual three sugars. He shifted in his seat and pulled his stuck arm up off the table. It made a ripping noise as it pulled off the dried milk puddle underneath.

"Exhausting," Marian replied. "So many babies! It reminded me of … of the daycare I used to work at." She coughed, stirred in her cream, sipped. She passed her napkin to Albert.

He took the napkin and put it on the sticky mess under his elbow, frowning. "Better watch it," said Albert. "Those little things are vectors of infection. Covered with germs. Like this table. On second thought, could you sit back a bit?" He waved her away with his hand and laughed.

"Oh, I never catch anything," Marian replied. And it occurred to her she didn't. Did immunity transfer with the soul, she puzzled? Mind you, the Black Plague wasn't around so much anymore. Her bout with polio back in the 40s had been mild, and it wasn't as much of a problem in the population as it had been. She speculated about shingles. She'd never had it, but she knew she must have had chicken pox at one time or another. Her childhoods were always harder to remember than her adulthoods.

She refocused on Albert. "Hey, did you get a community assignment?"

"Yeah. I'm not sure I want to do it, though. I'm supposed to act with community developers for the Africville community. Their first group meeting is Thursday. I'll see what it's like. It's not like I haven't already done tons of community development work. But Africville is interesting. They are trying to get ownership of the land they've lived on for years. Given the way our government treats our Native peoples, I don't have much hope."

"I heard about that," said Marian. "There were no titles to land given, right? They simply housed them, without ever surveying anything. And then unhoused them."

Albert nodded. "Part of the 'blacks are not people' attitude. I can't believe they still allow the situation to exist. Probably the city councillors know there are developers drooling at the thought of that land. Still…"

Marian stirred her coffee again to try to make it taste better. "I wonder how Dr. Rutgers picks the class assignments? Did the believers get the same community-type groups?"

"Not sure. Edwin and some of the others got assigned nursing homes and rural parishes. I'm not that keen on ministering, so I was overjoyed to be left out of those. They could have sent me to my home church." He shuddered. "Plus, they mostly have cars and can get further out of town." He shook his head. "I think I got this placement because I'm at least half black. No one else even seems to have a tan in our class. What's with that?"

"Suppose that assignment sort of makes sense. They might accept you better, maybe? With your experience and all. And I don't know about the pale people majority. I hate to think the college has a racial acceptance policy." Marian took a sip of the coffee, grimaced, dumped in another creamer. "Strong today." Marian drew a deep breath. "So, what do they need you to do there?"

"They want my support with effectively mobilizing protests. They've already covered the letter-writing and court challenges and the government hasn't done anything in response. So they feel it's time to take it to the streets. For some reason, they want my help." Albert shrugged. "And you know how Maritimers are about come-from-aways in general? It holds just as true with the groups in this city. Brown or not, I'm an alien in Africville. I hope they'll be able to use me. I've never led a protest before. I've supported them, sure, but I usually like to stay in the back. Never liked crowds much."

Marian nodded. "I'm with you! Too many people and things can turn on a dime. Scary. That's why I rarely go to church."

Albert laughed. "Marian, you're afraid of crowds—in church? Have you been lately? You can hear crickets."

Marian stared at him. "Really? Even at the Catholic Churches? They always seemed to have a crowd."

"Even the Catholics," Albert said. "Well, except on Christmas and Easter, of course."

"Wow. Who knew? I might have to go have a look at one of them. Purely for academic reasons, of course." Marian vaguely remembered pictures of the slaughter of her son and various other martyring in the old churches she'd attended. It made her sick at heart. She feared they were still there. "Listen, Albert, speaking of churches and other things—what's your view on reincarnation? They don't seem to cover that here. Do you ever think about it, or are you from the once and done school?"

11

Rebellious Child

"What, you mean the big end of times suck us up to heaven one? Or do you mean coming back as cockroaches or something? I believe Kafka was the end statement on that."

Marian pushed her mug away. "No, not cockroaches. Ew. I'm thinking about looking at reincarnation for my school project." She ruffled her hair. It stuck out like a crown with the static electricity. "Doesn't it seem a waste to spend so much effort on this," she circled her head with her hand, pushing down the more wild strands, "to have it all poof out of existence at the end?" She sat back in her chair and laughed. "I guess I'm hoping I'll see some return on my tuition money. Nirvana sounds 'groovy.'"

"Do we lose everything, though? I mean, there's got to be an accumulation of learning and all that. And the soul, of course. If you believe in that stuff."

"Right." Marian snorted. "The soul, okay. Maybe. But knowledge? As if anyone could keep track! People couldn't read and write for centuries, and so we lost all types of knowledge or changed it as we retold stories. Now people seem determined not to read or write. And what about the Mayans? Ancient Mesopotamia? China? Atlantis?"

"Okay, you're talking crazy now. Atlantis? What's in this coffee?" Albert peered into his cup. "Seriously, there must be lots of things passed on other ways—songs and recipes and art and all kinds of stuff. Like my dad teaching us all how to fish, with no instruction manuals, either. I'll bet your mum taught you how to sew."

"Sexist. Did your mother teach you to knit? Mine didn't teach me anything useful. Oh, except how to apply lipstick properly. Vital skill. She spent her time telling me to find a man for protection."

"Tada! And here I am, all protective and everything."

"Yeah." Marian grinned. "You're pretty fierce, you are. You're afraid of your coffee!"

"Only if it makes me see Atlantis. What I don't get is why the gospels surprised you so much. Didn't you ever go to church?"

"Never," Marian said. "Well, not for years and years." And years and years and years, she thought.

"And when you did go, you didn't listen, did you?"

"One of my main talents. Maybe my mother taught me that!"

"That's it," Albert said, "I need a new study buddy. Someone who," he counted on his fingers, "a. doesn't believe in an under ocean mystical city, and b. occasionally listened in church."

"Don't leave me with those Bible believers or I'll get you, bad. What would I say to them? They refuse to question anything! They'd probably spend hours praying over me. Already Elizabeth has offered to take me for a 'quiet herbal tea and a talk about your soul.' I think I'd need something stronger than camomile for that!"

"They're not that bad. At least, if you aren't offending them like you did in seminar today. Half the class crossed themselves and spat to prevent the evil eye."

Marian gritted her teeth. She'd made a mistake today. They'd been talking about the reading where Jesus had stayed back at the temple instead of leaving with his parents. A bunch of the students had blathered on about how Mary and Joseph should have understood that Jesus needed to be at the temple and just gotten over it. How it was proof that Mary was human, because she doubted God, or some such drivel. Apparently, loving your child wasn't one of those things divine persons could do.

Marian lost it. "That's not the way it happened. How can you possibly know what they were like? Or how that situation actually went?"

The class went silent. Marian was noticing her classmates going silent more and more often after she spoke.

Dr. Rutger chose this time to challenge her on what she said. "So how did it happen, Marian? Do you have another version you're reading? Do you know the Holy Family better than the rest of us?"

"Yes," she started, stopped. "I mean…"

Surprisingly, Dr. Rutger took pity on her and turned away to the chalkboard, drawing circles. "Marian has a good point, however. Reading the gospels as if they were news reports isn't correct. Someone wrote them well after the individuals involved were gone. There's evidence they altered some versions to match Old Testament prophecies, to help the new ideas be accepted. They changed dates and events and so forth. Created matching characters."

The students burst out into a mix of 'Word of God' rants

and general confusion, and many of them turned to glare at Marian. Their faces looked so familiar, like the ones she'd seen on the believers of all sorts in her lives. Damning faces.

Fortunately, the bell rang and everyone, distracted, left for the next class. Muttering.

12

In the Temple

Marian recalled very well the day they lost Yeshua—the fright and anger had burned deep into her mind. Miryam, Yoseph, family, and friends had made the group pilgrimage to the big Temple in Jerusalem for the Holy Days. The women packed and planned for everybody while the men argued religious issues and prepared themselves for the rabbinical discussions. Miryam, twenty-five, was carrying an infant and a pregnancy. Trying to keep track of the children was almost impossible with them running back and forth between all the families. It was an exhausting, hot trip. Finally, the motley group arrived in Jerusalem and set up camp, counted the kids, got washed and prepared. The men went off to pray.

Yeshua kept vanishing for hours and when he came back provided no explanation for where he went. Yoseph didn't keep track of him, either, focused as always on his own concerns. Miryam fretted as she cared for everyone except her firstborn son. There were strangers in the city for the Holy Days, and not all of them were trustworthy. She worried Yeshua might be hauled aside by a slaver or a Roman guard and sold or conscripted for the fleet. She warned Yeshua again and again, but he was in an uppity mood and just frowned at her and ran off. They spoiled the boy, she admitted, his obvious intelligence and handsome face making him a favourite of everybody. It caused him to become self-proud, and with puberty coming on, he had started talking back even to Miryam and Yoseph.

"He's off to see some girl," Yoseph chuckled. "Leave him be." Yoseph was elderly now and didn't fret over much lately. He still called Miryam to his bed, but she tried to get out of it. There'd been three babies since Yeshua, and he still appeared eager to breed as many offspring as possible. The frequent pregnancies exhausted Miryam, and she hoped he'd tire of her and take a fresh concubine soon. Yoseph was beginning to see through her frequent claims to being unclean because of her menses.

At long last, the Holy Day celebrations were over and the gaggle of friends and family turned towards home. The roads were full of bandits and Romans, so besides the melee of Yoseph's household, they intermingled with that of five other families. It caused so much confusion that they only realized Yeshua wasn't with them on the third day out.

Miryam wailed and pulled her hair. "My boy, my boy," she cried. "Where is he?" She begged Yoseph for a pony and cart to return to look for him. Grumbling, Yoseph and two his servants came with her. It took them a day and a half of fast trotting to arrive.

When they reached the Temple, who should they see but Yeshua, standing on a stool as proud as could be, so everyone could view him. He was talking to them about the Torah, answering questions for them. Yeshua had an unfair advantage, Miryam conceded. Many rabbis couldn't read, like Yoseph and Miryam, but she'd at least found someone in their village that could and had paid them to teach Yeshua. He'd learned on the scriptures and knew them backwards and forwards. Many of the rabbis had only memorized the key sections. So Yeshua sounded wise beyond his years. What astonished Miryam were the unusual responses he gave to the elders, good arguments that had even the wisest nodding. He clearly had thought through what he read.

She only had a few minutes to appreciate her son's brilliance because Yoseph, losing his patience, strode into the Temple and dragged him down off the stool by his arm. "Who do you think you are?" he roared. "You've worried your mother, disturbed your elders. Come away. It's time to go."

He yanked again on Yeshua, while apologizing again and again to the rabbis and elders in the Temple. He told them that Yeshua had been missing for days, that they thought the Romans had enslaved him or worse. He told them that his son wouldn't behave that way (only Miryam caught the implication), and he was so sorry for Yeshua's cheeky intrusion.

Yeshua pretended he didn't know either of his parents. He cried to the rabbis for support, told them he was being abducted, hadn't he been at the Temple for days, and didn't he need to be here?

The rabbis scratched their beards. "He is welcome to stay," one said.

"Mmm," the others hummed.

Miryam at first wept as Yeshua denied her. Her anger grew as the minutes dragged on. She stood to the side, watching what happened next. As a woman, she wasn't allowed to speak in the Temple. This always made her shake with anger.

The rabbis continued to growl. Yoseph blustered. Yeshua simply stood and poked at the ground with a stick. They questioned if Yeshua really was Yoseph's son. Yoseph dithered about the answer, not willing to concede to these strangers he wasn't or was.

Miryam, now enraged, wanted to slap them both. Finally, the men stopped arguing and allowed Yoseph to drag Yeshua back to Miryam. "Here is your boy," Yoseph declared, heavy-voiced, and stumbled back to the cart.

Yeshua crossed his arms and stamped his foot at Miryam like a petulant boy. "Mother! Let me live my life," he exclaimed. "I have important work to do. Leave me alone!"

Miryam felt a pain like a cloth ripping in her soul. She knew Yeshua would leave his home, and soon. He was already restless, absenting himself from the household, skipping tasks and avoiding responsibilities. He helped Yoseph build things, but only when asked. He kept running off to study with their rabbi.

She was furiously weeping. "Abandon your family? Abandon me? No! My heart can't bear it." She pulled her arms tight around her, shivering in the heat and frustration.

Yeshua looked in Miryam's eyes, seemed to see her more than he had for years. He rested his hand on her belly. "I'll come back with you, serve you until this one grows. After that, let me leave. I must."

Miryam nodded, joy singing in her ears. For all she knew, by then her family responsibilities would be over. Maybe Yoseph would be dead, and she'd be free. "Perhaps, then, I'll come with you," she added under her breath as they reached the cart.

13

Starving in Dubrovnik

D r. Rutgers pulled Marian aside as their next class started. "Are you okay? Sorry to put you on the spot. It wasn't fair to you. I wish your classmates would ask a question now and then, instead of taking everything as unquestionable truth. It reminds me of that line from the movie *Dogma*—you know, the one with Jay and Silent Bob?"

"Yes," Marian said. "I'm embarrassed to admit I love it."

He laughed. "No need to feel guilty—though the language! Recall how they praised ideas over beliefs?"

"Ideas can be changed, beliefs can't, or something?"

"Every time I see violence caused by religion, it spins around beliefs. And yet Jesus, Mohammed, Abraham, Buddha—they spoke about ideas. It breaks my heart sometimes."

"And we never seem to get past the hatred when beliefs are involved."

"Yes," Dr. Rutgers sighed. "Sometimes it seems like an uphill battle. At least a couple in this class seem a bit motivated to ask questions. It gives me hope."

Marian nodded, unable to speak. It was too familiar.

"So please keep questioning," he added. "Maybe we'll both learn something."

* * *

She could easily call up the many times religious hatred was directed her way, though she tried to forget them. Like when she was Miria, back in the barren Europe of the 1530s, trying to scrape together meals during the great famine. That life was cold, filled with hostility and hunger. She somehow survived through to puberty, formed small and bent-boned. Her family was Jewish and penniless, living surrounded by wealthy churches and a priory. The church members and priests dined well. Meanwhile, the needy of the village picked at grass and grieved as their animals and children died.

Miria's mother's sorrow filled her days. She keened about the miseries of being a parent of a daughter, not knowing Miria had experienced it many times. Her reincarnations were still confusing her, but Miria could sense deep in her bones what her mother cried about.

Then she watched as again and again her mother gave her children the tiny piece of bread left for her mother to eat. Shamefully, they ate. Later, Miria did the same for her own children. Mothers always ate last.

Her father tried going to the priory and begging for bread when Miria's mother was dying, but they turned him away with nothing. Jews didn't get much sympathy. They kept the Jewish families in a gated enclosure around the church in her town, and much of their scarce money was paid to the priests to lock them in at night. The priests told them it was for their own protection.

The Christians had just begun preaching that the Jews killed Jesus, forgetting that Jesus was himself a Jew. As they ranted, their parishioners took the sermons to mean that every Jew was fair game for maltreatment. Life became untenable. And short.

* * *

Even before that, she'd experienced the barbs of prejudice and hatred directed at Jews. Like in 1357, in Dubrovnik during the Black Plague, when she was Marya. That time she was a Jewish farm girl, living on the edge of a city, going out with the other women to slave over crops, returning home with their scanty results, exhausted.

When the plague started, the city people turned on each other like wolves, hiding in their houses and barring them to anyone the slightest bit different. Marya's farm group weren't Christian, so soon they couldn't sell their produce, and the women were slowly starved as the crops wintered over.

The richer families felt smug sitting on their unshared stored food, but rats raided much of it. Rats with fleas. The religious people, following Pope Gregory the IX and his madness about cats being the work of the devil, had killed all resident cats. The relieved rats were having a wonderful time, breeding, sharing fleas, bringing them and the plague into the city homes. So the rich became sicker than the poor. This enraged them.

The town leaders sorted the remaining villagers into groups by religion for quarantine, and even formerly friendly neighbours avoided sharing bread or any kindness. Anyone who could afford to leave the city fled to the hills. Those who couldn't, hid, locked in their homes, waiting to die, though the church sent quavering young priests to minister to them. So many people fell to the plague that they had to pile the bodies all over the fields Marya used to farm. Her former farming friends made a little money dragging the dead in carts through the streets to the outskirts, too tired to take them any further or bury them properly.

Marya worked as a nurse then, too, though modern nursing hadn't really been invented. People were still blaming infections on bad air, curses, the devil. Well, and cats.

Marya had learned to read by then. When there's no food to prepare and few children requiring care, there's more time to study. She found an aged medicine book and figured out what the squiggles meant by following an elderly priest about and asking him endless questions. She had to pay for that education, having two children by him, but initially no one seemed to mind. So many had died from starvation; life was more precious than propriety. The priest had been a kind and caring companion and teacher, and secretly provided food for her household while those less favoured were starving at the church gates.

Marya smuggled the donated scraps out of the old priest's priory and shared them as widely as she could until the Bishop's men found out and threw her into the street. Her priestly friend apologized, but had to obey his superior. He was told he wasn't allowed to feed the unworthy. Especially those Jews.

The Bishop kept Marya's children to serve in the priory which gave her the comfort that, though they would be slaves, they at least would be fed.

Marya knew she would survive. By then she'd learned enough medicine that villagers of all religious backgrounds paid her to be present at births, tend sicknesses, and heal wounds, and this meant she could afford food for her remaining family and herself. She could send her parents into the hills with the wealthy, where the air was cooler and the rats fewer.

The things she learned in her many lives kept her alive for a long time and taught her the value of an education. In fact, she often felt a shimmering pride as she healed her neighbours and brought home bread and meat. It reminded her of the old times when she'd been a midwife to Yoseph's clan. But now she knew even more.

14

Temptation

The term blew on. The winds rattling the windows of the residence turned hostile and wet. Sometimes the rain sounded like a giant was throwing fistfuls of rocks at them. The sun slipped away behind banks of fog, and the occasional bright hour had all the students skipping classes and running out to Point Pleasant Park to play football or walk.

Marian and Albert reviewed together, deepening their friendship. They felt isolated from the rest of the crowd, but as exam time drew closer, other students were more than happy to study with them, doubters though they were. The many evenings spent together in the residence common room built lay-lines of familiarity and trust throughout the class. The students shouted questions and references to each other between bites of pizza and shakes. Alfredo's, a shop at pizza corner in Halifax, knew their order—ten pizzas, three with donair sauce, three with garlic and oil, three with tomato sauce, and an extra-large with nothing but cheese. Toppings of all sorts. Plus six containers of dipping sauce and garlic bread. They'd gnaw through it all as they flung ideas about.

For a change of scene, they would often catch a bus to the Halifax Central Library, a huge glass enwrapped building where they broke up studying with long observation of the harbour ships or the downtown. Occasionally, they'd have a pricey coffee in the cafe on the top floor, but most of the time they snuck in reusable mugs filled with their own cheaper brew. Marian, Albert, Edwin and Donna, a minister from Montreal, took over one of the study pods and met there regularly, the soft enclosure making it quiet for them to hear each other and detangle what they were studying.

The travel back and forth cleared their thoughts and purged the scents of the increasingly foul residence. As studying got more involving, some of the students forgot to do laundry or shower. The towers of empty pizza boxes, decorated with drying leftover green peppers or curled up pieces of ham, added a distinctive perfume to the air, and garbage and recycle time was only once a week. It was good to get away from the miasma. Plus, the library bathrooms were clean.

Marian and Albert slowly became more affectionate than just friendly, and one long late study night after everyone else had left the common area, they found themselves in each other's arms. Kissing.

"Albert…" Marian pulled herself back, unlinked herself from his arms.

"That was nice," he said.

"It was. Wrong, but nice." Marian shook her head. "So easy to forget I'm married."

"Well, you're not, really, are you? You haven't seen him since August. Have you heard from him? No? So, what's the problem?"

"Still married." She wagged her ring finger at him. "No, no, no. Too much temptation here. I can't afford to lose my focus, can you? Do you know how long it's been since I was tested on anything? I have no idea if I can retain anything from the lectures at all. And my scholarship only renews if I get above a B plus."

Albert frowned. "Surely, all work and no play makes Marian a sad girl? Why not let these feelings we both seem to have for each other develop a bit? I guarantee I won't be distracting. Much."

Marian laughed. "Wow, that sure makes it a tempting offer! Non-distracting sex, with a side of guilt. Yep, that'll help my grades. Now, off you go. I've got more reading to do tonight and you ARE distracting me now."

Albert, show-pouting, gathered up his books. "It's not easy for me, either, you know. I haven't written an exam since undergrad. Besides, my dad is praying for me. Take about guilt! But I can find a little time for a little something-something now and again."

"Yeah, right. Because we aren't already isolated enough from the other students. Let's add an extramarital affair, eh?" Marian slapped her book closed, slammed the stack one on top of the other and shoved them under her arm. "I can just see that fundamentalist Elizabeth tightening her mouth at me and reporting me to the Dean. C'mon. Friends is enough. I shouldn't have allowed anything to happen."

She flung herself out of the common room and up the stairs to her place, sizzles of annoyance burning the air behind her.

15

Things Aren't Right

The next day, they spent the morning classes apart, heads down. Marian didn't ask her usual questions in seminar, and Edwin pulled her aside and asked her if she was okay. She nodded and avoided any more discussion. The last session of the day was in the tiniest classroom, and Albert squeezed in beside Marian, ignoring her glare.

"Friends? Fine." Albert gave Marian a shoulder-to-shoulder tap.

"Friends." She was relieved. If Neil ever found her, she did not want to have to explain being involved with Albert. She was sure he'd come out the worse in any fight. Albert was tall and well-muscled, but Neil was built like a linebacker, and didn't handle anger well.

She snorted to herself. There was an understatement. He handled anger badly! Like the day when the TV was snowy, and he picked it up and flung it through their front window. Or the time when he was furious that she was going out without him and he took the fireplace poker and swung it at the car, leaving dents and cracked glass everywhere. She couldn't stop shaking for days after that one. Of course, he apologized, bought her flowers, offered her a diamond necklace. Like he always did.

She was so glad to be elsewhere, hidden. She was even using a fake last name—Steeves was the name of the second-grade teacher she'd had in St. John. It was the first name she thought of when she applied for admission, typing it into her tiny phone as she walked the grocery aisles. She was afraid to let Neil see what she was doing.

Fortunately, the school was accommodating when she explained it all. They agreed to keep her real name hidden until graduation, but the Registrar looked at her seriously and said, "You will have to deal with this before then. Do you need someone to assist you?"

Marian fled, unwilling to discuss it further, nose clogging in readiness of tears. She never could handle people being kind to her over things. She'd devoted so many lives to being the strong, capable one, helping others. Being helped didn't come easily to her.

* * *

In the middle of exam revision, Albert led yet another protest on the steps of Province House. His group marched the short distance between it and Halifax City Hall, waving signs and yelling. A few of the protesters went off script and broke windows along Barrington Street, ruining the facade of a new condo building. Others started leaping on cars and threatening the drivers. Albert tried to stop them, but they wouldn't listen, calling out slurs at him. When the police arrived, he stood at the head of the group, demanding they imprison him first. It was a way to build trust, he told Marian later. She found it hard not to criticize him for building anger instead.

This was Albert's focus group's third or fourth protest, and the police had reached their tolerance limit. The protests were growing more desperate as time went on and nothing ever seemed to advance. There were lots of protests about a variety of injustices—rich growing richer while poor become poorer, missing resources in mental health care, violence by police towards the black LGBT community, lack of affordable housing—but destruction of property was a line they shouldn't have crossed.

One month of the police street checking almost every slightly tan student at Dal was what started this march rumbling along the street, and it resulted in every protester being put in jail. The police, furious with Albert's repeated presence, refused to allow him to access his course books while he was in hold waiting for the arraignment. He must have called Marian in a panic five times. They wouldn't let her bring the books to him, and the cops wouldn't even agree to pass them over to him in the cell. It was obvious they were hoping to make an example of him.

The courts were backlogged and although they had released a lot of the white students who could afford lawyers, Albert and the poorer protesters were still locked up. Albert eventually got out by agreeing to accept the blame for stirring up the group. His dad drove up from Shelburne to pay his bail. Albert ended up receiving three months' probation and a reprimand from the judge. The worst thing, he told Marian, was the disappointed look he got from his father.

* * *

When Albert returned to school, the other students hailed him as a hero, though Marian noticed they didn't offer to share their class notes to help him catch up. It showed all that messaging at the school about kindness and giving wasn't getting through when it came to academic competition.

Marian was glad she hadn't had that community assignment. The crowds and police would have reminded her of too many unhappy events. "Why wouldn't you stay in the background?" she argued to Albert as they photocopied her notes. "Save yourself and live to fight another time. Why take that responsibility on yourself?" Hide, just like she had always done, she thought.

Albert fumed as he stomped around the study room. "I wasn't the leader. I was just following Craig. He started everything—the rock throwing, the shouting at the cops. It was supposed to be a peaceful gathering. We knew the police were looking for a confrontation." He bashed the wall with his fist, dislodging a stained John Lennon 'Imagine' poster. "I should have stopped him. He got off easy, of course. He's been home for days."

"He's a white guy, right?"

"White and a friend of the mayor. This place! Everyone knows everyone, except if you don't, and then no one wants to know you. I'm so sick of being followed in stores all the time, especially if I haven't shaved." He flung himself into a chair, narrowly avoiding sending it backwards onto the floor. "That's why my dad went out to the Eastern Shore. Fewer cops to get in your face, even if you are brown. Here the cops'll arrest you if you're black and out admiring the roses in your own front yard. Reminds me of where I lived before."

Marian wanted to ask him where that was, try to calm him down, but Albert stormed past her out into the cold. The door thumped back in place after letting in a gust of freezing air. It sounded offended.

16

Hateful Men

Besides trying to study, Marian volunteered at the Compass group every week. When, as part of her contribution, she was asked to come up with a project, she taught some of the mums to knit. They'd only seen their grandmothers knit and were eager to pick it up. They spent a few weeks knitting hats for their babies and Marian made booties, working fast to produce a set for all the wee ones by Christmas. The mothers would sit curled over their knitting, tattoos flying as their fingers looped in and out around yarn and needles. Giggles and swears filled the air in equal measure as they lost track of their stitches.

The second week in November, Marian entered the church basement to find the group silent, Nancy grim. Lisa was absent.

She usually was the first to say hello to Marian. "What's wrong? Where's Lisa? Is she sick?" she asked, as she pulled off her coat and mittens.

Nancy patted the chair beside her. Marian sat, hands in lap. "They let Doug out of prison," Nancy said.

A chill ran up Marian's spine. As Lisa grew more comfortable with Marian, she revealed that her boyfriend Doug beat her regularly and hard. She had arrived with bruises on her arms and face a few times, and the group all agreed that Doug was out of control. The women offered verbal and babysitting support while Lisa finally gathered enough courage to lay charges against him. The police picked Doug up, and everyone thought they'd keep him in jail while awaiting trial. They hadn't.

Marian's experience was that men, once they were charged, didn't forgive easily. Or stop the beating. That often got worse. Her stomach sank.

Nancy continued, "Doug came to her place, despite the restraining order, and the police were too slow in responding. He hurt her badly. They had to admit her to the hospital. It's amazing he didn't kill her." Nancy sighed. "Now he's left town with their baby. The police are out searching for them, but no luck yet."

Marian scanned the women. Everyone was quiet. Not one spoke, there were no expressions of shock, no complaints. Their faces were set. She cried out, "Why do women let men get away with this? Wouldn't it be better to just live without them?"

A few murmurs slipped around the room like a heated draft. None were encouraging.

"She don't know."

"She a lezzie?"

"Nah, she's a nun."

"She not us, can see that!"

Marian blundered on. "Well, we should visit her! Where is she? She must be in such a state over Billy. Who's coming with me?" Marian rose, grabbed her coat "I can call a cab. A bunch

of us can leave in one and we'll get the driver to call another."
Everybody examined their shoes very closely. One girl bent to
re-tie her shoelace.

"I'll even pay for the cabs, both ways."

More congested silence.

"Maybe better we don't go," Brandy said. "It'll piss Doug off.
Maybe likely he hit her more."

Another mother, Amanda, a tiny girl with a wee pink baby,
scowled. It seemed wrong in all the pinkness. "My man didn't
appreciate me helping her with the report."

The other mothers nodded, held their babies tight enough
to cause protesting squeals. In the back of the room, a mum
shook a rattle, the sound sharp and startling.

"He has no right to be angry. And we're her friends. Aren't
we?" Marian's voice climbed a register or two.

Silence thick as fog.

Nancy stood up. "Well, if you aren't comfortable visiting,
maybe we can send her a card from us. I got out some card
making stuff out before you got here, Marian—it's on the table
there. Why don't we all write a note, or draw something, and
then sign it or make a symbol? Whatever's better for all of you.
Let's make it beautiful, too. The hospital is pretty ugly." As the
women got up and went to the table, she leaned over to Marian
and whispered, "A lot of their guys are in the same gang as
Doug. They wouldn't want to hear 'their girls' are speaking
against any of the gang."

Marian clenched her fists. When would women learn to stick
together? It was so frustrating! She stretched her tightened
muscles to loosen them, shook her arms out. "Well, then, I can
take it to her. I want to let her we're thinking of her, and no
one will get mad at me."

"That'd be great," Nancy declared, in a too-cheerful voice.

She sounded like Minnie Mouse. "She'll be glad to know that." She added in a whisper, "Don't say too much about the baby, in case…"

As if she would, thought Marian.

Only Nancy and Marian ended up signing their names to the card. Most of the other women made stars or hearts or faces or graffiti tags.

"It's not my real tag," Amanda admitted. "My boyfriend knows that one."

17

In the Infirmary

Marian carried the card to the downtown infirmary, an ancient place that a hundred years ago held the victims of the Halifax explosion. It was ugly and derelict and disheartening. Half of the wards were closed because of water leakage and mould. The government had said they would pull it down and build a new institution, but despite Albert's group and others' demonstrations, they had prepared no plans. When Marian asked for Lisa's room number, she was told she was on the gynaecology floor. Marian wondered what all had happened to her. Had he raped her in addition to the beating?

She scanned the hallways, passing old men on walkers scuffing painfully by and rooms where she could only see legs under blankets, hear the moans, smell the… She hurried on. When Marian at last found Lisa's room, around a dimly lit corner blocked by carts piled with laundry, she peeked in to see Lisa wrapped up in bandages and blankets, looking very young and small. When Lisa heard her at the door, she opened her eyes, stretched out her arms and wept. Marian ran in and gave her a lengthy hug until Lisa stopped quaking with sobs.

After she calmed down, Marian showed her the card which made Lisa cry again. Lisa traced each sign with her finger, saying the names of the group members—to her they were as clear as a signature. After counting her friends out, Lisa carefully folded the card and placed it under a pamphlet on Social Services in her drawer. She pushed other papers to cover it.

Marian watched, sadly aware that it would be safer for Lisa and her friends if the card remained hidden. Her heart broke. The world these women lived in was so hostile and dangerous. Even friendship wasn't allowed. "Now, how are you? Do you need anything? Can I bring you a real coffee?" she asked, rearranging Lisa's over-bed table. Marian bustled when she felt inadequate. Despite all her years of living, she had to steel herself to look at this young girl, beaten so desperately.

"Fine as kind," Lisa automatically responded, before bursting into tears again. "It's not as bad as the other time," Lisa said, after a moment, "when he broke my arm. That hurt so much! This time he only made bruises. Though," she hesitated, "he hurt me in other ways." Her eyes flipped wide open. Her pupils dilated and she fell back onto the bed.

The docs must have her on some serious medication, thought Marian. These shifts of mood don't seem natural.

"He took Billy! Where's Billy?" Lisa tried to sit up again but the pain and dizziness pulled her backward.

Marian held her hand. "I'm sure Billy's with Doug now and the police will find them. You know Doug won't harm him. He never has before, remember." She made her tone low, soothing. It seemed to work, because Lisa curled up onto her pillows and allowed her eyelids to flutter closed.

"You're right," Lisa murmured, "he loves Billy. He only ever hits me, not Billy. I know he won't hurt him. Doug loves Billy." It was like a mantra. She sniffed. "I miss him so much."

Marian sat, silent. Which did she miss?

"Do you know anyone who had their baby taken away?" Lisa mumbled, one eye visible.

She paused. "Yes, Lisa. It's awful. But it is so wonderful when they get back."

"Who was it? Did Social Services take their baby? How did they get him back?"

Marian knew why she was asking. Social Services likely wouldn't let Billy stay with Lisa if Doug was on the scene. She'd have to choose between them. She hesitated.

"Please tell me," Lisa pleaded. "I'm so afraid they won't give my baby back to me."

"Well, it was a long while ago, in Ireland, and it was my aunt." She mentally begged forgiveness for yet another lie. "Rules may be different here. The thing I remembered most is that she had to do exactly what Child Protection told her to do, even if that meant sending away someone she loved."

Lisa nodded, eyes large. She was completely stoned, thought Marian. She could tell her about Patrick and Lisa would forget it all.

"I… she had a baby boy. She didn't have a healthy pregnancy. She'd been drinking, and the baby wasn't good," Marian caught her breath. She still felt guilty, decades later.

"Oh, like a crack kid?"

"Yeah, just like that. She used to hang around with a bunch of people who drank a lot. When her little boy was born, he was all twitchy and screaming and wouldn't settle for me… her at all. She was going snaky in the hospital herself with no booze, so she checked herself out early."

"Wow. You don't sound like you came from that kind of family. You seem too good for that."

If she only knew. Some of her families were boozy, alcoholic, abusers and worse. She was murdered one time during a family altercation, way in Mongolia somewhere. Since then, she couldn't help a shiver whenever she looked at a knife. The feeling of her skin separating, the sensation of coming apart, the sudden, cold gaping, had never left her.

"She was lucky," said Marian. She hoped Lisa would think she'd dreamed this conversation. "Anyway, she'd drink and nurse Patrick, and he'd calm down. He must've been drinking some alcohol in her breast milk. But sometimes she forgot about him for hours. He screamed, but she ignored him. She often blacked out. And then he got tired and quiet. One day my... her boyfriend woke her up and said her wee one wasn't breathing normally. He was grey."

"Oh, my god. Did he die? Is Billy going to die?"

"No, no," said Marian, putting her hand on Lisa's arm, stopping the wail before it began. She wished she could talk to the doctor about Lisa's meds. "Her boyfriend drove her and the baby to the emergency room. The nurses had one look at him and her and called Child Protection. She was too high to realize what was happening until they stuck him into protection and her in jail, along with my... her partner. 'Failing to provide the necessities of life,' they claimed, and they were right."

"Yeah, like that guy they just sentenced, from Dartmouth. That is wild."

"She and her baby both might have died. She had a social worker visit her in prison. She was as kind as Nancy—she saw who I… she was underneath and thought it was worthwhile to work with her."

"I just love Nancy. She's the best." Lisa's soft voice was relaxing now. Slipping back down.

"Yes, she certainly is. Anyway, the worker persuaded the cops my aunt could give up booze and go to church, and told her if she stayed clean she'd be able to bring Patrick home."

"What about her boyfriend?"

"No, they didn't let him live with us. He had to leave. Part of the agreement." Marian glanced at Lisa, but she didn't see any reaction. "But my aunt didn't miss him as much as she missed Patty. She loved Patrick so she kicked the booze, even gave up smoking, so help me. The social worker got her a tiny charity flat."

"A flat? What's that?"

Marian turned her head away, swore. She was getting her lives mixed up again. "We were living in Ireland. They call their apartments 'flats.' Makes sense, doesn't it? They are flat."

Lisa giggled, high-pitched and just this side of hysteria. Marian lowered her voice, slowed her words. Cycling again.

"Anyway, after she'd been sober for six months, give or take, the social worker went to the priest and got him to vouch for my aunt so she could have Patty. It took another year and my aunt getting confirmed and going to Mass every single Sunday and Holy Day of Obligation and all, but I can still remember the day he came home."

"Did he recognize her?"

"Oh, no—he was but a mite of a thing when they took him. But I recognized him. I knew his sweet toes and the hair on the top of his head." Marian stopped, choking up. She recalled that time so well—the priest beaming, the worker watching her so closely, Patrick uncertain but smelling so good. She peeked at Lisa. Please God, whoever you are, let Billy come back to her, whole and healthy. She needs him, like I needed Patrick. Like I needed Yeshua.

Lisa, slowing her abruptly circling moods, appeared to have fallen asleep. Marian eased back against the chair. Despite herself, she slipped into her memories.

18

The Desert

After the rabbis returned Yeshua to them at the Temple, Miryam watched him like a goshawk. He kept to his word and stayed close, working with the others until his younger brother Matthew was working in the fields. Yoseph had long ago died of old age and Miryam depended on Yeshua and his brothers and step-brothers to help with the household. Matthew was a sturdy, unimaginative child, eager to work with his hands on the farmlands.

She was still unprepared when Yeshua turned twenty-one, he came to her and announced, "Mother, you remember your promise."

Miryam shrank. She wished she didn't. She hoped he'd forgotten. "Yes, I remember."

"I've studied all I can, worked with the family here for many years. I thank you for helping me learn to study, for letting me spend Sabbath with the rabbi and to travel to the Temple. But now it's the right moment for me to leave. I have something I have to do, something I can't do here, and I don't understand how to do it. I need to get away, to think."

Miryam couldn't speak. She couldn't swallow. Yeshua abruptly hugged her, kissed her, blessed her. And left.

That was the last she heard of him for thirty days. Thirty whole, awful, slow, silent days. No one knew where he had gone or what he was doing. Miryam, exhausted from weeks of crying, was lying down when the youngest of Yoseph's grandchildren danced into her chamber, singing, "He's coming, he's coming!"

"Who?" Miryam's heart leapt, but she squashed it. She'd given up hope.

"Yeshua. He's back! He says to tell you he's starving."

Miryam leapt up, tidied her hair, and dashed to the cooking building. "Prepare the finest lamb for supper," she cried. "Make all clean and bring out the choicest fruit and sweets. Pour the best wine. My beloved son has come back!"

The family gathered together a splendid feast though their food was still short. Some of the people grumbled, especially the older men who had struggled hard in the fields with Yoseph's other sons, but the muttering stopped when they caught sight of Yeshua. They gaped at him instead.

He appeared so different. He was gaunt, dirty, and barely able to stand, but somehow transformed. Jubilation shone from his face. He skipped around the family, lifting babies onto his shoulders, bowing before the elders. The children swarmed him, pulling him to the ground, climbing over him like puppies. When he spotted Miryam, he wept, pushing himself off the ground only to bend to kiss her feet. Tears streaked his dusty face.

"Dear mother. I'm so sorry I worried you. I needed a chance to reflect, and you let me. Truly you are blessed among women."

Miryam tugged him upward, hugged him tight, and wouldn't let go, though the children dragged him every which way. They absorbed some of the joy he radiated and exploded with it, laughing and racing about.

Over dinner, Yeshua told everyone how it had been out in the desert, the dehydration and the quiet, with fantastical tales of temptations by devils and more. Miryam watched, worried, fretted. She wasn't certain if he was telling the truth about the demons in the desert, or if he'd absorbed some prophecy from the scriptures he learned. Or gone mad, like his cousin John. Fasting for so long might have tumbled his mind. What was it he had to think about? He hadn't said.

She knew that his kinsmen were looking at him differently. They had listened to him teaching on the Sabbath before he left and watched him study. They knew he didn't agree with everything he learned and weren't certain how they thought about it. Their faces as he spoke were rigid and serious.

In the pit of her stomach, Miryam felt a prickling of fear.

19

Ireland

Marian dragged herself back to the present. Lisa seemed to be dozing, but when Marian rose to leave, she opened her eyes.

"Please stay, just a little longer? It's nice to have you here. Can you tell me more about your boy?"

Marian froze. Which one? Had she spoken out loud?

Lisa murmured, "Was Patrick a good boy? Did he get over being sick?"

"Oh yes, Patrick," Marian answered, in relief. "We all took some while to figure each other out, and that was tough. But we settled into a rhythm, like you and Billy will. We loved each other. He grew up so fast. I wish I was more present with him, but I was so busy trying to earn money for us."

"What did you do?" Lisa rolled over, tucked her hands under her head.

"I served in a pub. It was the only job I could get."

"Ooh. Good tips." Lisa shut her eyes. "Was he smart in school?"

"Decent. Better than some, worse than others. He became

mixed up with a bad crowd in middle school. Soon he was traveling about with the IRA."

Lisa didn't comment. Her breathing was even and deep.

Marian reflected on her time in Ireland. Her name then was Maeve. Memories swirled around her in a dark grey cloud. It seemed to her as if she lived this particular Irish life over and over again in her heart. She had so many regrets.

She took Lisa's hand, warmed it. Lisa was chilled through. Marian pulled the extra blanket over her, tucking it in about her shoulders. Lisa smiled a tiny smile, snuggled down. Marian's voice fell into to a slight Irish accent. "Lost him in the troubles, we did. My poor Patty." Lisa's eyes remained shut.

Maeve had encouraged Patrick to join the IRA. The group reminded her of the Judeans from the time before Yeshua, men fighting an oppressive force. It seemed a righteous fight. And times had changed. At least Patrick wouldn't risk being crucified.

She was right. They didn't crucify him. Instead, they shot him to pieces in Derry.

When his friends carried what was left of his body home, the protestants followed and beat her within an inch of her life for harbouring him and his allies. After that, the grief and pain was so intense she slipped back into drinking, and the flu and malnutrition soon carried her off. She didn't regret that one bit. She wasn't fond of that time. It still filled her with shame. She vowed to do things better in her next reincarnation.

* * *

Had she? She couldn't recall. She'd lived so many lives, memories felting together like woollen fibres. Sometimes she could tease out a particular strand, gaze at its colour and texture, but often things seemed so tightly intertwined they appeared a muddy, solid fabric.

Marian shook her head. This Bible reading and analysis had shaken her memories loose, or maybe her age was catching up with her, untangling those strands. Would this happen with next year's Islamic studies as well? Could she control those spinning thoughts? She better watch herself or they would put her away for 'assessment.'

She had that happen before. Did not want to do it again. In one of her lives—she didn't remember which—a fever made her talk in Aramaic. They locked her up in a madhouse to force her to stop talking to herself in 'voices.' When she continued, when she shouted louder, they soaked her in ice baths, starved her, stuck her in a lonely place with no windows. That time, too, she chose not to extend. There are easy ways to end an uncomfortable life—get chilly, stay chilled, die of pneumonia. Relatively painless. And quick when you are already weakened with illness.

* * *

Marian stood as softly as she could, gently straightening the blankets over Lisa's now-sleeping form. She quietly clicked off the overhead light and pulled the door almost completely closed. Lisa needed an undisturbed sleep. Walking past the nurses' station, Marian leaned over the half wall and stage whispered. "Lisa's asleep. Room 309."

A young nurse glanced up and smiled. "Thank God. She's been so restless. I probably shouldn't tell you this but you are her only visitor, so I figure you must be close? The police called—they have a lead on her boyfriend. They are going to pick him up now."

Marian breathed out. She hadn't realized how tense she was. "Any word about the baby?"

"Yes!" The nurse broke into a wide beam. "Such wonderful news! They hear he's with the father and still fine."

Marian waited in front of the elevator, gazed upwards. "Quick work," she said to the ceiling. "Almost makes a girl believe in you."

The elevator motor chuckled in response.

20

Trying to Keep Focus

"Exam day tomorrow!" Albert moaned. "Can you believe it? I'm nowhere near ready."

"You must have a crappy study buddy," Marian said, laughing. She felt so light since the police had returned Billy to Lisa, as if someone actually answered her prayers. That hadn't happened too often over the years. Marian always wondered why. Wasn't she following the rules? Didn't she help set the rules up? What was she doing wrong? Did they change them and she hadn't realized it?

"Do you think they prefer us to regurgitate stuff? Dr. Rutgers says no, but he's not the only marker. Some of them have absolutely no sense of humour. Like Dr. 'Toothy.' She won't want us to write anything but what she told us, verbatim, from Confessions."

Marian was in her flannel pyjamas, fuzzy slippers and all. She couldn't believe she could walk all over campus in her pyjamas and coat and boots and no one cared. At least half the college was dressed as if they never got out of bed these exam revision days. It was comforting, like the Kraft Dinner they had all started to survive on.

Albert still dressed in 'grown-up' clothes. He put them on every morning, pressed them every evening. Marian told him he needed to loosen up. He disagreed, saying he could focus better in proper clothing. It wasn't helping his nerves. He hunched over his books like a gargoyle, barely speaking to anyone, knees jumping.

"I don't know." Albert fiddled with his page tabs. "I'm so worried about Smyth's open book exam. I swear they only do that so they can make the questions harder." He ran his finger over the book, bristled with post-its. "I think I have too many flags," he added.

"Have you figured out your project for next term? You've been awfully secretive." Marian stepped up behind him, ran her finger around his ear and down his neck. Albert shivered. "You can tell me…"

He pulled away. "Yeah. You'll steal it and say it was your idea. Now quit distracting me or I'll fail for sure."

"We could work off that tension."

"Ha! Infidel! Whore of Babylon!" Albert pushed her hand aside. "Fine for you. I've still got at least a couple of hours of hard slogging. I keep getting Matthew and Mark mixed up."

"Unsurprising. That's why I appreciate John."

"You just like John because he has Jesus hang out with women, not only special men."

"Well, he did!"

"And we know this how? No one else mentions it."

Marian stuck her tongue out at him. "Oh, go study. I'm making a cuppa—do you want one?"

"Lovely, ta," Albert said in the faux British accent he assumed when discussing tea.

Marian wasn't sure she liked that accent. It made her wonder what other weird snobberies lay under Albert's good guy exterior. She shuffled into the kitchen and filled the kettle. Waiting for it to boil, she found her past life intruding again.

21

Meeting Magda

Yes, Yeshua did prefer the company of women, she remembered. The brothers were constantly after him to fight, to be big and noisy and startling, to stir the pot. Yeshua chose to be quieter, or did at least until his final arrival in Jerusalem. So he sent the men on ahead to locate places to stay while he wandered and chatted with the women. Miryam figured that's how he fell in love with the Magdalene.

Yeshua, Miryam, many of their kin and various disciples and hangers on had been roaming for months. John's former admirers were with them, too, given to clutching Yeshua's robe and praying at him. Sometimes families would join in, carrying their sick or almost dead relatives, begging for healing. Their death smells and moans added a whole layer of misery. It was a noisome, unruly throng, and it was always difficult to locate places for them all to stay.

A significant clutch of smiling women also journeyed with them. Yeshua was so handsome, and he spoke with everyone in his gentle voice, an irresistible combination. Miryam at first wondered how many shared his bed. Her son was a vigorous young man, and the girls were more than willing. It would have been tough for him to refuse their comforts. Miryam spotted some of the men taking advantage of their association with Yeshua to score a few bedmates. Love and lust and pregnancies were springing up here and there. Once again, she was grateful for her training in midwifery.

All of them in the mob seemed to suspend real life for this stage of roaming. The crowd followed Yeshua; he talked and taught and ate and slept and didn't argue, just went on. He helped the people they found along the road as they travelled, sharing food with them all and passing his hands over the suffering. Those people would also join the group, and the crowds kept following him.

Sometimes Yeshua would call on Miryam and other healers for advice with the sick they passed. Other times he treated them himself—he'd studied Miryam's ways and learned medicines and techniques. Occasionally he would pray over them. It didn't seem to matter what he did. If it worked, it seemed miraculous. If not, the people still sang his praises for trying. Men weren't often healers.

Miryam laughed to herself. If she healed them without Yeshua next to her, they'd give her a fish or some bread in payment and that would be the outcome to it. If Yeshua did it, there was a full song and dance. Fewer payments, but lots of noisy praising. In the end, Miryam preferred the fish.

One day as they were trudging on another long unexplained slog through Dalmanutha, a strange woman joined the gathering. After a few days of walking in the back, she forced herself through the crowds to be near to Yeshua. When they stopped for a rest, she threw herself onto the ground in front of him and hugged his feet. This impressed Miryam. They'd been going a long while without baths, and she swore she could smell Yeshua's feet from a distance. This girl was serious.

He leaned down and gently pulled the woman up to standing. She was almost as tall as he. They whispered for a moment, looking at each other, intent. Miryam saw something change in Yeshua's face, a fresh glow. He led on, but he wouldn't release the woman's hand, nor she his. They chatted as they went, a lengthy, private conversation they didn't invite others to join.

By nightfall the full group was gossiping. Two women stomped off, angrily bickering and gesticulating, their hopes dashed. Two men tried to pull the new woman aside, but Yeshua frowned and they retreated. The men clustered about, hoping to talk to him themselves, but this time, he didn't pay attention. He was completely engrossed with the woman, whoever she was.

At long last, they came to a river and stopped and make camp. Miryam summoned the stranger, found out her name. Mary from Magdala, called Magda, joined her at the river to bathe with the other women. Miryam gave her a good look-over as she did. What she saw, she liked—lengthy, strong limbs, athletic shape, breasts to nourish many a babe. She approved even more when she heard Magda talk. Her speech was deep and melodious and she used a vocabulary that showed she was from a well-to-do home.

So when Magda and Yeshua slipped off into the dark away from the fire, Miryam smiled to herself. Her son needed to marry, settle. Then he could become a teacher and cease this endless rambling. He and Magda and Miryam and her other children would form their own household and Miryam could spend the rest of her life bouncing grandchildren on her knee and spoiling them. She would be able to stop worrying.

The next day, practically quivering with excitement and plans, she asked Yeshua how he slept. He blinked at her through sleepy eyes.

"Magda and I spoke all night," he said, his tone rough and dry. "She truly believes in me, in what I must do. Few do. Not even you, mother."

"You only talked? Such a beautiful woman and you only talked all night? I am in despair!" Miryam made to pull her hair.

Yeshua grinned and held her hands. "We promise to wed as soon as possible. Surely you agree we should wait for that? We'll get a rabbi the next time we stop."

Miryam didn't know quite how to respond to this, so she remained quiet. Her son had apparently stayed innocent, despite all the temptations. Miryam had no notion about Magda's past and didn't care. She could see the affection shimmer between them.

She chewed on his comment that she didn't believe in him as they tramped along. Would she have walked all this way if she hadn't? Her feet were worn to the bone! She would have been angry, but she was entirely too weary to hold any emotion but the wish her son would find happiness.

In the next town, the rabbi was delighted to marry the two and a few of the other travelling couples. This was probably because Miryam supplied him well with their best wine and arranged for the ceremonies to happen before Yeshua started his preaching. She fretted that the rabbi might not agree once he heard what Yeshua had to say.

Simply to be annoying, Miryam was certain, after the weddings Yeshua spent an hour ranting against wealthy men and declaring they couldn't get into heaven. Miryam ground her teeth. Here was a happy event when they could have relied on hefty donations, and he offended all the people in the comfortable town. The rich men got up and left, complaining to each other, declining to leave any money behind. As usual, the followers ended up with small rations and no more wine until their next stop.

She vowed to review some of the other lessons she and Yeshua had created, the caring for each other lessons, the sharing lessons. Their entire crowd was starving, and a little sharing along the way might ease the frustration. Miryam often heard angry muttering back in the ranks.

22

Discovering Mary

The kettle screamed, unnoticed, until Albert came into the kitchen and shut it off. He peered into Marian's face. "Are you okay? Didn't you hear the kettle?"

"Oh, sorry. I was mentally flossing."

"Flossing what? Seems serious if you can block out that awful noise!" Albert poured the water into the teapot, swished it around, poured it out.

Marian smiled. He did know how to make a proper pot of tea. "Nothing much." She paused. "Just my project."

"So, when are you going to tell me what it is?"

"Not till you tell me yours," she taunted. "Oh, what the hell. Actually, I am writing about Mary. Or Miryam, as she they called her back then."

"Really? How very Roman Catholic of you." Albert grinned. "I thought you didn't go for that church?"

"I don't. What self-respecting girl could put up with all that unquestioning misogyny? They have Mary all wrong, and for some reason it really bugs me. They've spent centuries making her into this superhero wax figure product who goes about oozing pure thoughts, and nothing else, all the time. Who do you suppose washed Yeshua's poopy pants, for god's sake? Wiped his snotty nose?" Marian waved her hands in agitation.

"Ew. Literally." He tossed three tea bags in the teapot, added the water.

"Anyway, I want to straighten out a few things. I feel kind of sorry for her, after what they did to her. She was a real flesh and blood woman at one point, you know."

"Well, good luck with that," Albert said. "From my experience, people go a little frothy when it comes to the Blessed Virgin Mary. Do you remember that Jesuit who came in for the guest lecture?" He poured two cups, handed one to Marian.

"Mmm," she said through a sip of tea. "Hot."

"Who, the Jesuit?"

"The tea, silly. Though the Jesuit was hot, too. Extremely, unbelievably good looking. I wonder if they recruit for handsomeness? I've never seen an ugly Jesuit, come to think of it." She blew on her drink, her eyes dancing. "Mind you, that guy got pretty sweaty and bothered talking about Mary, didn't he? I wanted to go away and leave them alone together to finish up." She frowned. "You're right about the frothing, though. I better pick my advisers carefully."

"Yes, I'll have to figure out about that, too. I'm considering researching all the similarities in the gospels. It's just like gas prices. I sense collusion."

"You do realize," Marian said, smiling at him, "They'll tar and feather us by the time we're done."

"I think you'd look rather lovely as a budgie," replied Albert, resting his hand on her shoulder for a moment. He gave her a long look that had yearning all over it and took his tea back to his room.

Marian put her feet up on the other chair in the shared kitchen, sipping her tea, puzzling over the Mary cult development. She recalled going hunting for works about herself some years before and being repelled about the way her name was being assigned to miracles, babbling streams, unpleasant situations like plagues and battles, even bizarre things like slices of toast. It made her seem bigger than the big God and yet more kitschy.

After reading some of the books written about her cult, she was grateful not to be in heaven, if it existed, what with all those prayers being constantly sent to her. Demand upon demand. That Rosary alone would be deafening, what with all the Hail Marys. And appearing all over the place! War zones. The tops of mountains. Jungle grottoes. It sounded exhausting, not heavenly at all. Being eternally caring and endlessly calm seemed more hellish to her.

About the only book she read about herself that she liked was Diane Schoemperlen's *Our Lady of the Lost and Found*, which at least gave her cute sneakers. And let her be tired, and in need of a rest.

23

Mary is Everywhere

She was in Japan that time when she first became aware of 'her' cult. Then she was Mariko, living quietly and going to temples to appease the Kami. It was fascinating studying the religion and the culture there from behind the scenes—she hadn't had a Japanese life yet. The gods seemed to be easily appeased: be clean, give them some rice and water, and they would leave you alone. Except occasionally, when they were terrifying. Were they the cause of the frightening earthquakes? Mariko prayed constantly to her household god to save her from them. Somehow she knew they'd be how she died and sure enough, a quake and a fire and she was off to her next generation.

Before that, she started to see Jesuits in their black robes insinuating their way through the villages. They brought their Mary with them, and soon pictures and paintings and idols of the Virgin showed up. Simple drawings, extensive lacquer work, even oil paintings. She would have felt self-conscious, except that none of the portraits looked at all like her. They were all white, so pale they looked unwell. Their Jesus was visibly hydrocephalic. It made Mariko ill. He'd had a big head, she remembered with a wince, but it wasn't as if he was born a tiny fully formed man with a head larger than hers.

The newly converted in Japan to related to Mary better than the gruesome Jesus crucified that the brothers also insisted on carrying around. Many of the Japanese had been on the receiving or giving end of torture, and they shied away from worshipping it. Mariko's mother dragged her to a few of the Christian ceremonies and she saw how they presented Mary as a kind, gentle contact with the divine. Mary, the loving mother, the virtuous and always unscarred young girl—they understood and spoke comfortably to her. Women wanted to be as desired as her. Men dreamt of her, ever the precious virgin. The perfect female.

She snorted. A mistranslation, Marian had read in one book. The Hebrew word 'almah' actually meant 'girl of childbearing age' as well as virgin. And all unmarried women, with children or without, were called almah. It was particularly funny given the general behaviour of many women and men in the decades just before Yeshua's birth. Sex was, briefly, a positive thing then. So many women got pregnant by a variety of men they had to change the inheritance rules to matrilineal. This worked for a while until the men re-created laws and more dogma to hold women in place.

Mariko didn't get to hang around long enough to witness how the Japanese Mary adoration worked out. By 1560 she was shaken and burnt and was off in Africa being reborn in a malaria-laden jungle.

* * *

Sometimes these transitions made her reel. In the jungle, she spoke Shona, and they called her Ruva, for flower. When she again became aware of her surroundings, some ten years later, she found it hard to believe she was there. What was she meant to learn here? Surely there was some reason why she'd been flung into this dangerous place?

Despite her initial confusion, she passed a long and peaceful existence and bore several children, five of whom survived. By the day she died, she was as wrinkled as an old fig. It was a marvellous and refreshing break from official religions. It felt so useful to follow simple routines and superstitions, most of which were practical, based in survival in the natural world. Worshipping a river seemed entirely proper when without the river the entire clan would die.

She learned her purpose when she discovered multiple medicines from plants there. The roots of a plant helped control the fevers of malaria, so she shared it with the people in her village, helping many of them. They sought her other medicines, and again she played midwife to half the local women. She even had other healers to work beside her. Nobody criticized her or abused her or accused her of being a witch. Life was hard, and straightforward because of this. No one had any energy for plotting evil. Sometimes, now, Marian wondered where she lived in Africa—they had had no idea—and if her tribe was still there. The village probably altered when it became a colony. She sighed. Nothing good ever stayed the same. Perhaps you couldn't even see the stars there anymore. Maybe they had a Mary cult now, too. Maybe she appeared in a jungle vine.

It was enough to make her want to move to Antarctica.

24

Exams

The next day, the exam hall was silent except for the whirr-clicking of the electric clock, the almost audible smells of sweating unwashed students, the freezing rain pelting against the windows. Thoughts seemed to fly through the air, nebulous ribbons, fleeing the student's heads and pens. Some could almost be heard crashing to the ground, as the students sighed and shifted on their chairs.

Dr. Rutgers sat at the front of the room, typing furiously and silently on his iPad. No clicky keyboard for him; no idle moment, either. He was working on a book and said he was way past deadline. Once in a while Marian felt his gaze. He glared at her for a moment, then slid his glance over to the next student, checking each one. It was as if he was scanning their brains, finding them wanting, and moving on to search another's. Was it Marian's imagination he looked more often at her than at the others? Did he think she was cheating? He sure wouldn't when he read her answers. Who would try to cheat this badly?

Edwin, the keenest pupil, was a full half hour early to finish, stretching up tall and carrying his paper to the front desk in front of him like a choir singer. Marian peeked over at Albert. His head bent, he was writing quickly, flipping pages over and back as he filled every space. It didn't look like it was going well.

Marian wrote her final sentence, stabbing the period with unusual ferocity. Done, she thought, and put her pen down on the desk. She'd said every single thing she could remember and process. Looking at the clock, she cursed. She'd finished in the last fifteen minutes of the exam period, and that meant she'd have to wait to leave until everyone stopped writing and the exam time was over. The college supposed this kept things quiet for the students finishing up, but it always led to pen-tapping and the rustling of papers. Unable to help herself, she carefully leafed through her test book, looking for any mistakes, but her brain was woolly and tired and empty. She craved sleep for about a year. Her next exam was the following morning.

Finally, Dr. Rutgers stopped typing and announced there were ten minutes remaining to finish. He stood up, stretched and started to collect the completed exams.

The clock pinged for the final five minutes and still Albert scribbled away. Marian, nervous on his behalf, jiggled her leg until Dr. Rutgers loomed up behind her and made her jump by clearing his throat.

He finally called time and Albert and four other students blew out the air in their respective chests and flipped over their papers. Dr. Rutgers ambled over to pick up the booklets, then released the class. They fled, barely taking time to put on their still soggy coats.

"First exam in so long," moaned Marian, once they got

outside the building. "I'd forgotten how hard they are."

"Don't even talk to me," Albert grumbled. He sucked in a chestful of fresh air, shook his head. "You finished way early."

"Hey. That's because I had nothing to write." They looked at each other, glum. "Hope I passed," Marian added. "I don't want to have to experience that one again." They dragged silently back to the residence, avoiding the other students. Again, Marian wondered if this whole thing was a mistake. Why was she studying the times she already survived? She could barely keep straight what she had endured and what she read for the course. She hoped she had stayed in the present for the exam. Her memories kept crowding front and centre often now, and often she got confused.

25

John Causes Trouble

One exam question had been about John the Baptist, for example. Marian remembered thinking he was odd even back when she was Miryam. She assumed his problems were from Elizabeth getting pregnant so old. Miryam had called on her in case she wished to rid herself of the babe, but it was too late by the time she reached Elizabeth's home. And Elizabeth herself was bursting with excitement, as if the baby was divine instead of a colossal mistake. She'd stayed with her until the delivery, but it was nerve-wracking. Would the baby be whole and healthy? Would she deliver safely?

The delivery went smoothly, all things considered, but neither baby nor mother seemed right after it. John ended up being a strange baby and a savage child, given to night terrors and colic, restless and loud. The family shunned him at gatherings, the other children wouldn't play with him. He yelled and leapt around, making everyone uncomfortable. Only Yeshua could calm him and spend time with him as if he was a normal child.

Elizabeth was besotted, waited on him hand and foot, smiled at his every utterance. Nauseated, Miryam was glad to get out of that house and return to her own.

When John grew into an adult and left to live in the wilds by himself, clad only in furs, Elizabeth created a fabulous cover story for him. Those visions? Not insanity, but God speaking to him. The sermons and threats? John was merely casting out devils. The restlessness? He was responding to God's requests. Elizabeth was so efficient at creating this image that they built a following of other misled mystics who brought him food and wine and listened to his harangues by the hour. His sermons grew with the crowds.

Miryam wouldn't have minded this, or his wild ways, except for what he did to Yeshua. Miryam had wanted to check in on her aging cousin, and John fascinated Yeshua, so the two of them had left the family behind and headed to Qasr el Yahud. John and Elizabeth were camping there on a stormy day, rare rain falling on the desert ground.

As soon as they arrived, John, by then a huge hairy monster of a man, pulled Yeshua through the crush toward the lake where he was baptizing the gathered people. They hugged each other, exclaimed in joy. Then John thrust Yeshua under the water, and right at the same time, the sun broke through the clouds and streamed onto the landscape. The people oohed and ahhed. John used the scene as part of a lengthy rant about how Yeshua was the chosen one, the son of God, the Messiah. The crowd ate it up, pushing toward the spluttering Yeshua and almost drowning him by trying to touch him.

John may as well have signed Yeshua's death warrant right then. Talk started at once amongst the men about how they should take back their homeland, now that their Messiah had come. Others begged for Yeshua to heal them, pulling at his clothes, tugging on his arm. One of them stole his sandal. Another ripped out a bit of his hair. He started out smiling at every person who attacked him, but soon his smiles took a desperate edge. They were hurting him.

Miryam, furious, cried to Elizabeth. "What is John doing? Doesn't he realize what he says will run back to Rome?"

Elizabeth smiled a calm and scary smile. "We lack a leader. Leaders. Why shouldn't it be John and Yeshua? They could rule, you know—look at how they are in the palm of John's hand! The people would follow them anywhere, even into battle."

Miryam twisted her hands into fists in indignation. "But the Romans will crucify them! It's not the right time to draw their attention. Do you want John dead?"

Elizabeth continued to smile, patted Miryam's arm, once, twice, three times. "We'll lead beside them. Queens of the Holy Land. We'll have servants, fine clothes, and all the figs we can eat. Think of it!"

Miryam stared at her cousin in shock. "Our sons will die, Elizabeth. They'll torture them, kill them. Remember the Judeans? What are you thinking?"

"They'll be martyred, you mean." Elizabeth gazed at Miryam, her eyes glassy. "Our sons will be even stronger as martyrs, don't you understand?"

Miryam drew back in horror, pushing her way through the swarm to her son. "We need to leave," she said, "I'm unwell." In truth, she felt like vomiting. The image of Daniel dying on a cross hung in front of her.

Yeshua glanced at her, at the massed crowd, ran a hand over his bleeding head. "You're right. We should leave. It's not time." He put his arm around her and they squirmed their way back through the mob. It closed behind them like a river as everyone pressed forward to John, hoping they, too, would receive God's blessing.

"Foolish, stupid bleating sheep," Miryam declared, frowning, as she stamped her way up the hill.

"Lambs," countered Yeshua, limping along beside her on his one sandal. "And all still unknowing. Pity them, Mother. They know not what they do."

"Well, it's time for them to learn," she said, still furious. "They were pulling your hair out!" Miryam added to herself, "Besides, some foolish ones do think they know what they're doing!"

Yeshua was deep in thought and didn't respond.

They returned to their kinsmen, but not long after that Yeshua started his wandering and preaching. Miryam blamed the 'divine blessing' John gave him at the lake. Several of John's followers started to hang around, waiting for Yeshua to come out for a walk and they'd join him, blathering, gesturing, and demanding food until Miryam cheerfully threw them out of the family compound. Every time they came, the crowds got bigger, and Miryam feared for them all. She sent her other sons out to search for news, to find out how the Romans were taking this upstart preacher John. Were they planning to destroy him? Them all?

For a while the news was good. It seemed their rulers had little interest. They were off campaigning and the new queen had taken a fancy to John, enjoying his muscles and wild looks. Miryam didn't know how she saw that through his reek—he stank like a rancid camel despite all his bathing. Herod Antipas invited him to his palace to amuse his new wife Herodias, and she was pleased at first, thinking that this was a sign Herod finally wanted her to be happy.

John, not the least bit grateful, spent his time there continually shaming Herod for divorcing his original wife and marrying his brother's. John howled and 'cast out demons,' especially from the wealthy, until everyone at court was thoroughly fed up. It was unpleasant having your sins called out in the middle of supper. Damaged the digestion.

It couldn't last. Soon, someone, probably Herodias, ordered John beheaded for his behaviour, and the Centurions, often the angry recipients of John's judgements, promptly killed him without charge or trial. Miryam so wished John had played along with Herod and Herodias until he could escape the court with his life. Instead, he kept annoying everyone until he wound up with his head on a platter.

Elizabeth, refusing to grieve like a normal mother, at once campaigned to have him declared a martyr, and she was successful. John became so much bigger in death than he'd been in life—everybody was talking about him, telling of miracles and blessings. The flocks that followed Yeshua grew larger and mobs of John's followers changed allegiance and gathered behind Yeshua.

Miryam was afraid. She watched Yeshua more closely for signs of madness and resolved that from now on, she would travel with him. It was heady stuff, this mass adoration. She worried Yeshua's head would turn, and he'd fight, as everybody seemed to wish. She knew if that happened it was likely he'd end up skewered or with his head on a dish like his cousin. So many people had been crucified already, left rotting in the heat.

Some said the smell from Golgotha blew all the way to Egypt.

26

Christmases Past

Albert and Marian dragged themselves through the last three exams. Most of them were less challenging than Dr. Rutger's—just memorization of stated beliefs and political structures—but that was hard enough for their tired minds. Their last test covered the Confessions of St. Augustine, where the Coles' Notes were, fortunately, unusually good. The course itself mirrored a Coles' Notes discussion. Professor "Toothy" Grant, annoyed she had boring St. Augustine to teach, muttered about wasting her time on first years and refused to tolerate any analysis.

Marian and Albert often skipped her class that fall. They'd wander, beside the rocky waterfront, reusable mugs in hand, letting the constant salty winds blow the sleepiness and conflicted thoughts out of their heads. Then winter came.

"You know that Newfoundland expression, right?" Albert yelled once, when the winds blew too icy for a casual walk and they were hustling down the street back from the cafe, heads bent and scarves wrapped tight.

Marian looked at him, head tilted. "Which one? I know

about a hundred!"

"Git outside and let the wind blow the dirt off ya."

Marian grinned. "I've heard a different version. Today I am purged of everything. I can't feel my legs!"

"Chicken. Shall we retreat?"

"Please. I am over-refreshed."

They found an empty corner by a classroom and sipped their coffee there, the warming steam helping them reawaken their frozen lips. Gradually they peeled off scarves, mitts, coats. The chill seeped through the windows, so Marian wrapped up again. Albert just shivered.

"And to think I moved here for the weather!" Marian joked.

"Good job we came inside," said Albert. He pressed his nose against the foggy window. "The sleet is starting. Again."

"Still don't want to go to class. She's so boring. We might as well just read the Confessions and get it over with." Marian said.

"You haven't studied the Confessions yet? What a slacker! No surprise you are still such a heathen."

"What's your excuse, then?"

"I've only read the Coles' Notes? It's pretty dull, too. And it seems Augustine feels what was good for him is sufficient for everyone else. Galling. Speaking of annoying, when exams are over, would you like to go out on a date?"

"A real date?"

"Well, we did have... something... before exams, didn't we?"

Marian shook her head. "I don't know, Albert. I'm still married, I'm the scholarship kid, I can't mess things up. I'm actually finding most of this," she waved at the classroom, "interesting. I think it's better if we stay in the friend zone."

Albert blinked his eyes for a moment, then nodded. "Well,

friend, how about we do Christmas together, anyway? I've booked a cottage—we can read novels and eat toasted marshmallows and everything." He saw the look on Marian's face. "As friends, honest. I just can't stand another Christmas with my family going on about 'One day that will be you up there!' in church. They are so set on me being a minister. It's like I really have no choice."

Marian felt a lightness fill her. She hadn't been looking forward to Christmas spent in her room. "That sounds great, Albert. Let me pay for half the cottage, though."

"Ah, we'll settle up afterward. After all, I know where you live."

* * *

Marian's memories of the many Christmases she'd endured were not generally positive, and she had avoided all church services in this life until arriving at the college. Churches, shopping malls, large groups in enclosed spaces frightened her. She'd witnessed madness in crowds so repeatedly that the thought of being entrapped in a building with a group of zealots was alarming. They could turn on you so quickly.

She had the experience of Yeshua's death to establish her terror of crowds. Her fears got worse when she was Moyre, in Massachusetts colony, back when Puritanism was still present and strong. Moyre was born that time to progressive parents in Boston. They believed in the Unitarian movement, along with many of the country's founding fathers. Moyre's mother was a healer of sorts, although she avoided being seen practicing after the witch trials in Salem. She did what she could to settle things down—like forbidding rye bread, figuring the mould that grew on the flour was the reason for the damning visions. Sometimes people even listened to her. As Moyre grew, she followed her mother on her still-permitted midwifery rounds, carrying water and cloths and cuddling the newborns, hugging their wrinkled bodies and keeping them warm.

The church in Massachusetts was terrifying for a little girl. The Unitarians held their services in a large dark hall, and the colonial leaders gathered took turns discussing religion in loud voices. How many people were in God, they asked of each other, thumping their fists on the tables when they didn't agree. Was Mary real? When was Jesus made holy? Endless arguments, every time they went.

Moyre wasn't a tall child, born once again during a post-war famine, and the preaching men loomed large than gods and twice as loud. At least they acted kinder than the remaining Puritans, who demanded that their women give birth without pain medications from Moyre's mother's box. Sometimes they sneaked the mothers a dose of pain-reliever despite the men's objections, but always in secret. Eyes were watching. Eyes of hateful men.

Marian remembered all of her own births, many in pain, fewer not. Sometimes she'd be tiny, and the babes grew big; other times she'd be lucky, and the proportions were reversed. Pain didn't make the child or mother any healthier or stop the babies from coming, and Marian didn't see the need for it. One time, after a baby tore Marian from front to back as his head crowned, she could not look at him. She felt such resentment as she healed, incompletely, leaving her miserable for ages. Fistulas were awful, unclean, and hated. She gave thanks that she wasn't living in a country where she'd be expelled into the desert.

27

Escape

The sensation of needless pain came back to Marian after exam week as a literal flood of Norwalk virus flushed through the dorm. Everyone was sick. Even illicit pet goldfish in the residence sickened and died. The bathrooms smelled of diarrhea; the halls reeked of vomit, the bedrooms stank. So many students and staff fell ill that Public Health became involved. They slapped the whole place under a quarantine and trapped everyone in the mess's midst.

Marian felt like hell, up every half hour, passing classmates going to or from the bathroom. She saw several students praying, but she was more inclined to curse as she writhed. The residents kept reinfecting each other since the Norwalk germs and their relatives weren't kind enough to share immunity. The college administration arranged the delivery of Gatorade and electrolyte solutions on Marian's recommendation and ordered a boxful of hand sanitizer from Amazon. Marian set the bottles everywhere and washed her hands so regularly they were red and raw. The acrid smell of alcohol gel hid the other odours.

After consulting with Public Health, the school administration agreed to allow them to leave once they had stopped vomiting for two days. As the days passed, one student, then another, escaped to the outside world, deemed Norwalk-free.

Albert crept by Marian's room after the worst had passed and most of the students had left. "Are you still alive?" he croaked, from the doorway.

"No. But I can sleep now," Marian whispered through cracked lips. She poked her head out from under her blankets.

"What's the news on the quarantine? Can we escape?"

"One more day and we're sprung. Still game for the cottage trip?"

"Yes please! Fresh air, trees, no profs, no vomiting students—heaven!"

* * *

Later, following much laundry and many hot showers, they loaded a rental car and fled south to a series of winterized chalets nestled by Kejimkujik Provincial Park. The Mersey River gurgled beside the cabins and tumbled along ice ledges attached to the shores. It was a peaceful, clean, and cozy paradise, and they spent hours wandering by the riverbank, playing pooh-sticks, clearing out their lungs and sinuses. They roasted marshmallows in the wood stove, did a jigsaw puzzle. It was perfect for decompressing.

Tossing another log on the fire, Marian joked, "This is the second-best Christmas I've ever had." She toasted her palms.

"I don't understand why we celebrate now, anyway. No one knows the correct day." She was there, and even she didn't know. Miryam and Yoseph were on the road and she wasn't paying much attention to dates as she staggered along between contractions.

"The banality of statutory holidays," answered Albert, in a gloomy tone. He shut his eyes. "It's always all about bureaucracy and advertising seasons. And Santa."

Marian plopped onto the sofa beside him. "Did you believe in Santa?"

"Yes, for ages. Sometimes I still do. What about you?"

"I had a super practical father. Didn't believe in lying to youngsters, so I never had Santa Claus or the Easter Bunny or church. Made me real popular in kindergarten when I told everyone Santa wasn't legitimate."

Albert winced, eyes still shut.

"My mum tried to sneak things in for us, fill up little stockings, but he caught her and tell on her, every time. For years I thought I had been terribly awfully bad, and that's why Santa never came." Marian closed her eyes, too.

"How terrible," Albert said. "Did he at least read you fairy stories?"

"Nope. He used to read me old Bobbsey Twin and Swallows and Amazons tales."

"Not even Narnia?"

"Not even that."

"No wonder you never had kids. No fun in your house—must have dreaded recreating that."

Marian laughed. "No, it wasn't that bad. We had fun in other ways. We camped and made crafts and took photos of flowers and animals. He taught me to paint and draw. We did tons of stuff together. He just preferred we got excited about the natural world over the commercial one."

Albert put his arm around her. "You were lucky, then. I had

to make toys out of used straws."

"We lived in a box…"

"In the middle of the road… went to work before we got up."

Marian laughed. "I love Monty Python."

"I do, too. But right now I'm thinking there's something else I cherish." He kissed her, his hands running through her hair. "It's chilly here," Albert suggested, "Maybe we should get under the blankets, curl up. To preserve heat, mind."

28

Antonio

As they dozed, curled up together, comfy and warm, Marian thought about the last time she'd felt so close to a man. For so many of her lives, affection had been unattainable. She figured she was being punished for not loving Yoseph, for not being able to keep Yeshua from self-destructing, for not being pure enough. Her heart deadened, her spirit broke as one loveless marriage followed another.

She fell in love, once, in Mexico. She was called Maria then, living between the Mexican-American wars in Teocelo, a small gathering near Xalapa. The Mary cult was alive and well in her village, thanks to the Spaniards who settled there, and her parents named her after the village's patron saint. Every year the men would dress a statue of the Santisima Virgen Maria in garlands and parade her through streets on their shoulders. Maria's family celebrated her birthday then, joining the celebrations together.

In that time, she adored Antonio. The youth had black curly hair, sparkling brown eyes, and an impossibly adorable dimple. His family lived next door, and he and Maria spent their childhood making up games and playing hide and seek in the market. One day, as Maria walked home from shopping, carrying melons and corn, someone whispered her name.

"Maria, Maria, come here."

"Who are you?" The voice seemed to come from the back of the village hall.

"Come see," the voice said.

Maria smiled. She recognized the voice now. Maria ran behind the building and surprised him. She tapped him on the shoulder, and he whipped around, alarmed, then grinned.

"Sneaky!"

Maria giggled. Antonio stopped her laugh with a kiss. It startled Maria, but it was a lovely kiss. Warm, enthusiastic and no longer from a playmate. Asking, but not expecting.

She answered yes, kissing him back with passion. The produce spilled from her hands as they sought his torso, as they touched each other, held each other tight.

They wed the next week. With the war threatening, everybody married as quickly as possible. And everyone agreed Maria and Antonio made a wonderful love-match. They moved into the rear room in Maria's house and didn't appear for three days, talking and making love and sleeping and making love again.

The villagers were scandalized and then thrilled. When they emerged, the people beamed at them, staring at Maria's stomach as if expecting a baby to spring out immediately. It didn't take long for the villagers to have a reason to smile. Maria became pregnant, and Antonio grew even more tender to her, all while strutting around the town like a cock-of-the-walk.

He travelled much of the time, training for the war, but when he arrived home, he would bring her trinkets and exotic drinks and glow at her, as she did at him. Surrounded by tenderness, Maria easily gave birth to a dark-haired, brown-eyed baby girl, Angelica.

Maria woke each morning with Antonio on one side of her and Angelica on the other. She shimmered with happiness.

Two weeks after Angelica spoke her first word, Maria awakened to find Antonio gone. They had called him up to fight. She filled the gaping hole he left with prayers and service to the church.

Despite her pleading, the war took him. It consumed him. She never received a body to bury—he'd fallen somewhere far away, and they'd buried him in unblessed ground. Maria could barely stand her anguish. She looked to Angelica, found Antonio in her eyes, clutched her to her chest. They entwined themselves together for many months, unable to move forward. Maria spent hours in the church, praying for Antonio and demanding to know why he had been taken from them. No answer came.

Angelica fell ill with a virus that weakened her, and a cholera outbreak ended her short life. They inscribed Angelica's name and Antonio's on the headstone as if they buried Antonio beside her, but soon they needed to carve another name.

Maria was alone again and pregnant. Perhaps it was her unhappiness, but this pregnancy went badly—the baby made her so sick she couldn't eat and she wasted away, bit by bit, with hunger and illnesses. The village stopped smiling at her and instead avoided looking her direction, fearing her sickness could spread to their own families. Maria's mother, hooded with grief, spent entire days praying in front of the Mary statue after they confined Maria to bed. When Maria started to have seizures, no one saw them, or called for help. And so she recycled again.

* * *

The morning dawned fresh and bright and ice-cold. The fire had gone out. Marian wrapped her blanket around her and wobbled out to load up the wood stove. She was just getting a flame to flicker at the edge of the kindling when Albert appeared at the door to his bedroom.

He scratched his arm, yawned. "Hey, you're good at that!"

"I should be," answered Marian. "I… um… was a guide."

"So many skills," Albert nodded approvingly. "I admire a girl who knows how to wield a match."

"Less of the 'girl' thing, mister. I haven't been a schoolgirl for years."

"Meant as a compliment. You don't look a day over twenty." Marian set her teeth. "So, boy—what are we up to today? Got any plans already in place?"

Albert sat heavily on the futon. "I've got a proposal for you."

"Bring it on," Marian said. She made a last poke at the logs and shut the stove door. Still shivering, she stumbled over to join Albert.

"Well, you see, my parents were furious I didn't go there for Christmas. There was talk of tying me to one of John's lobster traps for the next dumping day."

"Dumping day?"

"Don't you ever watch the news? Dumping day is the day when all the lobster boats race out to dump their traps and claim their sites. Absolutely terrifying. I went along once and nearly caught my foot in a rope as the traps were being spun out. Saw my life pass before my eyes." He coughed. "'It was really boring'..."

"So, the parents were fairly angry, then?"

Albert nodded, glum. He got up and opened the stove door, unnecessarily stabbing at the flames, almost putting them out. "See, I had to calm them down. Especially my mum, who actually cried over the phone."

"Sit down. The fire is fine. So, tell me what you did?"

"I kind of told them I'd be down after Christmas. We'd be down. That I was spending time with you, first."

"Wouldn't that be more upsetting? Wasting time with a friend instead of with the family? My parents would have burst into flames."

"Well... I did add something about you and I being in a relationship and our need to spend some time alone togeth—"

"Relationship! What? Assume, much?"

Ducking his head, Albert said, "I know, I know. But mum was crying. Crying! I had to do something." He sniffled. "So of course she invited you up, too. A sort of rom-com Christmas in the country thing. I'm so sorry." He went to fill the kettle. The water splashing against metal was the only sound for a few moments.

"Oh, my god. So now they are expecting us to fall in shiny new love under the mistletoe?" Marian crossed her arms, swaddled her blanket tighter, and scowled. "First of all, I hate those movies. Second, I am beginning to hate you. What gave you the right to tell them all this without even checking with me?"

"She was crying... There should be a law against mothers crying. It turns me into mush." He poured the water over the coffee grounds. "Oh, by the way, you might want to watch any swearing when we get there. My mum gets right in your face if you do." He frowned. "You wouldn't want that. She's scary when she gets mad."

"So now I am expected to watch my words in front of a terrifying woman while I pretend we have a 'relationship'? This sounds like a grand way to end our vacation. Thanks ever so!"

Albert brought over two cups of coffee and a pleading expression. "It'll be fun, I promise. Shelburne is so pretty at this time of year, and my brothers are cool. They… um… think we are getting married."

"What?" Marian stood, sloshing coffee on her legs. She brushed at it with her hand. "Dammit. No. Just no. Take me home."

"I can't. It would take too long. We're supposed to be there for lunch. A big family-all-together lunch."

Marian stared at him for a full minute. Sighing, she gave in. "Well, I'll go visit for your poor weeping mum, but I am telling them we are just friends. And you owe me big time." She walked to her bedroom. "Don't think I won't collect."

Albert smiled. "Counting on it, actually," he said softly.

29

Shelburne Family

The drive down was quiet, very quiet. Marian spent it looking at the scenery and muttering under her breath. This area of Nova Scotia was plain ugly, she thought. Nothing but scrub trees, thick enough to block the sea. The car swerved around the winding road, making her nauseous. From time to time she would shoot baleful glances at her driver.

Albert knew enough not to speak.

When they arrived in the actual town of Shelburne, Marian was surprised to find herself charmed. She hadn't been to this part of the province before, and the town was all prettified up with Christmas bows and lights. Her mood lightened. They were probably nice people, and the prospect of a home-cooked meal was heartening. How bad could it be?

Albert slowed the car to gesture at a white church with a rounded tower on the top. "That's the church my folks expect me to 'lead.' See the exciting places all around it? Or not." He slowed to a creep. "Quality of life, as versus quantity, eh? Like, for example, the major hangout is over there—the Legion.

Along here is my family's local, the Ship's Sinking."

The town had a few tired shops with drooping Christmas ornaments and 'sale' signs and a littering of more white clapboard houses. The harbour opened a street away from where they were driving. Marian pushed down her window, breathed in the air. The smell of seaweed made her smile.

"Shut that! It's freezing!"

"Poor boy." She closed it. "Needed to smell the sea. For strengthening purposes. So, where does your family live?"

"We're right on the edge of town. The suburbs." Albert risked a laugh. "Not that this is much of an 'urb.'" He turned left, then right, and pulled up at another white house.

Marian was thinking she would easily get lost here. Everything looked the same. Even the Legion was in a white clapboard house. Maybe there was a rule?

"Here we are," Albert said in a hearty voice. "Parents in the mirror may be closer than they appear…"

He wasn't wrong. The front door slapped open and a thin grey-haired woman flew down the front stairs, waving her arms. "Albert, Albert!"

Albert looked over at Marian. Marian faked a smile. The woman was wearing an old-timey, probably vintage apron. Already Marian felt like she was slipping into the past, something she hadn't done since exams. At least this past was also her past from her parent's life. Like the 1950s.

Albert's mum tugged open the door on Marian's side, almost pulled her out of the car. "And here you are, Marian! Albert has told us so much about you."

The rest of the family poured out of the house. They mobbed Marian. Everyone seemed to want to squeeze her and yell greetings in her face, even the family dog.

Eventually she was allowed to leave the hugs and pull away from Albert's mum and dad and brothers and dog. They all pushed her toward the open house door.

"Come on," Albert's dad called. "It's colder than a witches' tit out here."

The wind was taking the frigid temperature and changing it to an arctic one, so Marian didn't hesitate. She crammed herself into the tiny entrance hall and tugged off her boots, tucking them into the closet.

Albert's mother bustled toward her, holding slipper socks. "Now that we can talk properly, let me introduce myself. I'm Beth. The old guy over there is Harold. The boys can introduce themselves. Here—put these on. The floor is kind of cold since himself," she nodded at Harold, "hasn't gotten around to putting in the extra insulation."

"You know I can't get down there with my back," Harold grumbled.

Marian felt a laugh bubbling up. Christmas movie, here we come, she thought. We've got the aging parents who need help, the Christmas decorations, the large brothers lounging attractively all over the place. None of them appeared to be married, or at least didn't have a partner with them. It was a good thing, too, she figured, as she wedged herself into the crowded dining room. Never mind, this Christmas movie changed it up a bit. The person being asked to return to the small town was a guy. The plot points could be interesting. She pulled in her stomach and managed to sit down.

"I'm so happy you could join us, Marian. Maybe you can persuade that guy to come up to visit more often." Marian nodded, winked at Albert.

"Oh, isn't she cute? She winked at you, Albert. No one winks anymore."

"Sit down, Harold, and don't frighten her off. Come on, boys, let's get started. Everything is just ready."

Beth ran on skinny legs back and forth to the kitchen, passing out lashings of Christmas leftovers. The table was completely covered when she finally sat down. "Oh dear, I've forgotten grace in all the excitement. You say it, Albert. You need the practice."

There was a disgruntled pause, but after a moment, Albert mumbled a grace.

"You're going to have to talk louder than that, son, if you want them to hear you at the back." Harold added, "The church has a great sound from everywhere but the pulpit. There's a story about that..."

"Which we will hear later. Now, tell us all about you." Beth leaned forward, eyes bright. "Albert told me you're the only one he can talk to at school."

Marian blushed. "What else did he tell you?" She scraped her fork across her plate. "Did he mention that I'm married?"

It was as if a bomb went off in the middle of the dinner table.

"No, dear, he forgot that detail." Beth frowned at Albert. "But you went to that cottage together."

"Mum!" All the boys protested.

"As friends," Marian said. "We're just friends."

Beth glared at Albert. "We'll talk later." She reached a hand across the table to take Marian's. "You are welcome here no matter what you are."

Sure, thought Marian, half an hour later. As soon as she'd denied being Albert's fiancée, the interest of the family towards her turned mechanical. Instead, the family focused on Albert. His calling. The manse at the church.

"It's draughty and ugly inside," said John, "but we could fix it up in no time at all. A few licks of paint and it might be the sort of place I'd hang out."

"Of course," he looked at Marian, raised his eyebrows, "it would benefit from a woman's touch."

Marian swallowed what she wanted to reply.

"Boys," Beth stood, gathering up dishes, "The water heater seems cranky. Could you have a look at it while Marian and I do the dishes?"

30

Future Plans

They escaped the 1950s by about four in the afternoon, after so many references to Albert's future career that he was red-faced and steaming. They never asked a single question about why Marian was at school with Albert.

After they loaded the remainders of lunch into the car, John ran up and peered in the window. "Albert, I know it's hell here, but you've got to come back here to live, soon. Mum and dad can't live on their own without someone to check on them."

"And you can't? Lobster season is pretty short. You've got the whole rest of the year to play good son."

"I'm not the golden boy. They love you best. They are literally existing for your first legitimate sermon from that pulpit." Turning to Marian, he added, "Our mother's family has had a pew there since the 1800s."

"Look, John, I'm not even sure I want to be a pastor, let alone one in this hellhole. Lay off. I don't owe you or anyone else." Albert slammed the car door, shutting the conversation off.

* * *

The drive home was thickly silent, laden with unsaid criticisms and complaints. Marian opened her window a slit to blow the bad air out. Around Liverpool, she'd had enough.

"Look, that was harsh. Aren't your parents paying for your tuition? And they are getting older."

"Thanks, I hadn't noticed any of that." He slapped the steering wheel, making Marian jump. She still found sudden noises terrifying.

"Sorry. I can't even think about going back there. Dad only got his job because of mum—otherwise they don't hire black people anywhere. Did you know they shipped a whole lot of the Loyalist settlers to Africa back in the day? I'm pretty sure they'd do the same thing now. Bunch of racists." He took a swallow of water. "Mum thinks they will let me be a minister here. She's wrong. I smell the burning torches now. It's only gotten worse as the younger crowd move away."

"But everybody seemed so nice," Marian exclaimed, feeling foolish as quickly as the words left her mouth. Maritimers generally 'seemed' nice, but that didn't mean they didn't slash you bloody the minute your back was turned. "But your parents—they need you, don't they?"

Albert snorted. "I stayed home and looked after them for years. I've repaired everything that can be repaired in that shack. I worked at the godforsaken gas station until it closed, doing my undergrad course by course. It's time for the other guys to take a turn."

"But..."

"You don't know. Your parents are gone. My burden gets bigger and bigger every year. They refuse to move out of that house—did you see the stairs? The clutter?" Albert shook his head. "Nope, I'm done. I can only be there for a short time before it gets to me and I'm afraid I'll say something that will hurt them."

Marian kept her mouth closed, but she wanted to comment that being rejected by their child would hurt worse. She knew.

31

A Window Opens

Marian and Albert arrived back at their residence tense and unprepared to deal with the new term. Other classmates had paired up over the holidays and the common room was suddenly full of twisting, trysting shapes.

The Norwalk must have tied them closely in suffering, Marian laughed to Albert.

Albert moaned. "Don't remind me! Unnameable parts of me are still sore..."

Their classmates had the gaunt look of people who needed a good feed. It was doubtless the dark closing in so soon in the day, but everyone trailed down the halls like wraiths, unnaturally pale. Afraid to touch any of the light switches or faucets.

Somehow they reconnected with their studies. It was time to begin work on the major projects they needed to finish the year. Albert remained secretive about his topic. He'd changed his mind, he told Marian. He wanted to process it.

* * *

Marian decided to let him wallow. She had bigger fish to fry. She girded her loins and met with her advisor, Dr. Rutger, the second week of the term. "I've got my thesis planned," she announced as soon as she stepped into his office, trying to sound certain. "My proposal is to revisit the biography of Mary."

Dr. Rutgers scratched his chin. He didn't blanch or wag his famous scandalized eyebrows at her or anything. Instead, he said, "I hoped you might."

"You did? Why?"

"Well, there's your name. And your in-class comments. They are a clue." He beamed a surprising smile at her.

"O-Oh, S-s-sorry. Didn't realize I was so obvious." She wasn't understanding this whole scene. Why was he acting so creepy? She plopped into the office chair, sending some photocopied papers slipping under the desk.

"There is also your ancestry, Miryam." He lifted his 'Jesus, Wow!' coffee mug and drank deeply.

Marian paled. "My name is Marian."

"Yes, now, but before you were Miryam, weren't you? And Maria? Mariko?"

Marian felt faint. "What...?"

Dr. Rutger cleared his throat, traced a line with his finger on the desk. Marian had seen that before, but where? She gulped, confused.

Dr. Rutger, after a moment's hesitation, went on. "At the start of term, I worried that you'd recognize me right away, let out our secret. Not that you have the other times we've crossed paths. You made no signal. Then, I assumed we might connect through the class. We didn't. I realized I had to sign up as your advisor and contact you directly myself, reveal who I truly was. Perhaps now we can end this reincarnation foolishness."

Marian stared at him. There it was, something strange and yet familiar. "It can't be—you aren't—Peter?" Her head spun. She reached out to hold on to the desk. It, at least, felt solid. "But I heard they martyred you! Didn't you earn the special heaven pass?"

"Strange, that hasn't helped me at all. I'm sure I am still paying off those three denials. Dammit. I wish I'd confessed I knew him and been crucified right beside him. Maybe then I'd be in paradise now, instead of dragging through life after life here." He grimaced. "Did you get to experience the Black Plague? Yuck. Oozing buboes everywhere. And then I was stuck in Australia for ages. Barely a dingo to keep me company, and all those spiders! They wouldn't even bite me, just crawled all over me, no matter how I begged them to kill me or leave me alone." He sighed, pulled a wet-bar-sized bottle of bourbon out of his bottom drawer and poured the contents into his mug. "And what about India—right during the war for independence? I swear I saw you there. Dead bodies and guns and smells… Hasn't it been exhausting?"

"But you teach… all those lies?"

"I used to fight it," Peter replied, spreading his fingers wide on his desktop. "But, those gospels weren't meant to be a literal translation, as you know. It was about the narrative, the love. The story was the framework. I try to talk about that, about the 'is-ness,' as one of my profs called it."

She balled up her fists. "Fine. So, according to you, I was meaningless? Except as a walking womb? What about the work I did to raise Yeshua, form the message, create the church?

What about all the people, all over the world worshipping Mary, that came to believe through me? Doesn't any of that count? Do I mean absolutely nothing?" She pounded her fist onto the desk. A mother-of-pearl rosary slithered to the floor. It made her shimmer with annoyance. Really. A bit of respect, please.

Peter barked a laugh. "Do you expect if people knew you and all of what you did, they'd love you any more? Does any child rejoice to learn his parents are Santa Claus? They already adore you now. What more do you need? If anything, we've had to tone down their Mary-worship over the years." He frowned. "At least you don't have to be played in Passion plays everywhere as the bad guy, the coward who abandoned our Saviour. That is so galling. When will they let that go? It's been two thousand years!"

Marian looked at her feet. Would it make a difference to the Blessed Virgin worshippers to see she wore dirty thrift shop boots in the snow? Probably not. People viewed her as a unique woman, perfect in all dimensions. Reality couldn't compete. Their Mary doesn't do laundry. Their Mary wouldn't have suffered through Norwalk, fled an abusive marriage, been so angry. Their Mary was a shiny clean white porcelain statue. And what was more important? Her person, or the message she'd conveyed? She no longer knew.

Marian rubbed her palm over her face. "I still want to study her as my project. What if I broaden my research, review the literature again, work to get a grip on the evolution of the Mary cult? Maybe even understand it myself. Do you think that might help me stop reincarnating, too? I am beyond exhausted."

Dr. Rutgers, Peter, shrugged. "I don't know. Maybe that would help us both. I must be missing something, or I wouldn't continue coming back. I feel awful. So tired—as if all my lives have stretched me out until I'm almost transparent. Thank heavens the students still see me or I'd feel as ephemeral as that plastic bag blowing about the harbour." He flapped at the window as the bag danced past, then frowned again. His eyebrows collided together in the middle of his face. "Miryam, what if this is all there is? Endless reincarnation until there's nothing left? Can you imagine if there isn't a heaven? After all we've told people? They swallow it all, without question, even the hateful bits I work to expunge. Total sheep."

"Lambs," smiled Marian. "Little lambs, remember?"

Peter waved a dismissive hand, took a deep breath. "Well, I'm glad you and Albert are friends. In this class of 'lambs.' Tough to make connections with our doubts, don't you find? And you two have so much in common."

Marian fidgeted, wondering. Was Albert another reincarnate? It couldn't be. He never said. Dr. Rutgers didn't clarify.

"This course, though—it's setting off my visions." Marian wrapped her arms around herself. "I worry the whole class will assume I'm babbling and commit me. I've no idea who or what I am half the time."

"I know how you feel. That's why I initially chose to teach religion. It seemed like the best method to corral the remembrances. Then I found out I had to exactly follow the accepted syllabus. It's troublesome to keep everything in order." He paused. "Maybe after you are done, you can walk the same path. You seem more interested in learning than preaching. And you write well."

Gee thanks, she grumbled. Only 2000 years of practice, give or take. "You could be right. Not sure if I want to spend another life teaching, though. Besides, I'm still annoyed about how you men wrote Magda and I right out of the narrative. I'd need to revise that."

Dr. Rutgers nodded, closed his eyes for a moment. "Not surprised. You always tried to speak truth to power. I still recall you telling us off after he died. I wondered at that time if maybe you should have been leading us. You were always the organized one."

"I was never a leader. I prefer the rear benches. I'm safer there."

"That was my argument and here we are. Maybe we're supposed to take a little risky leadership? I haven't taken much initiative in my teaching, sadly. Afraid to lose tenure. Still, it's a living." He laughed. "Have you said anything about your experiences to Albert? You look like you're getting to be friends."

"No! I still relive the burning in my dreams. Not keen to repeat that. He'd likely think I was a witch or worse."

"Understood. I'm not a great fan of the upside-down crucifixion, myself." He gathered up his books. "Well, I'm off to burn bridges. I think it's time I corrected a few misunderstandings." He waved a binder at her. "My book proposal. It's about a few things that I know will be viewed as scandalous. But if I can't speak up now, after all this time, what's the point? They can't keep on misleading people in this way." He stood, walked toward the door, turned to look back at Marian. "I think you should talk to Albert about all this, though. He might surprise you. Might be a support for you."

Marian sat, breathing hard. Why did Peter reveal himself? Why now? In one respect, it was a comfort to run into someone who knew her son, the times they'd suffered through. On the other, she was astonished that Peter had been recycled like she had. Peter was favoured by Yeshua back then. She thought he'd have a direct line to heaven, if there was such a thing. She wished she could spend hours with Peter, but more talk might reveal their past, and the effects of that would likely be disastrous. Maybe they'd slip into their past personas and end up committed again. She sensed that his speaking to her meant something would shift, but what? Was the time coming when she going to die?

Marian hoped not. She was still enjoying this life, would like it to continue for a while longer. Most of all, she didn't want to have to put on another life and start again. Crossing her fingers, she vowed to be careful as she walked around. She sent a silent prayer upward to whoever. "Please. A little longer. Let me discover what you need me to learn, so I can quit this."

<h1 style="text-align:center">32</h1>

<h1 style="text-align:center">Love and Distrust</h1>

Marian couldn't wait to go to Compass after the winter holidays. She'd missed the laughter and joking, the cuddling of babies. She could do real things there, diapering babies or teaching a recipe, things that wouldn't require her muddled brain to put angels on heads of pins. When she arrived, many of the same women were there, even Lisa and Billy, who was crawling now. They'd all brought New Year's presents for Marian.

Nancy said, "They wanted to bring you some presents for Christmas, but you were all tied up in the quarantine. So they decided we could celebrate Ukrainian Christmas instead."

Marian, surprised, felt the tingle of tears at the back of her eyes. They brought her stick-on tattoos and skull earrings, so "you can look just like us." Pens and pencils and hair tie-backs and other things for school. All dollar store or thrift store stuff but dearer for that—Marian knew how short their money was.

She just about fell apart when she saw they even managed to bake her a cake, complete with a Christmas tree decoration. Nancy supplied the ingredients, and the women baked it and did the frosting. They'd frozen it while she was away. "We were going to do a cross, but that seemed too depressing," Lisa said.

Marian agreed.

She hugged them all, squeezed the babies, got covered with the icing. Laughter raced around the room and she felt wrapped in love. And yet, what had she done for them?

"I feel as if I get more out of being here than I give," she said to Nancy.

"Me, too. I am so honoured to be a part of their lives. Trust isn't easy for them."

Later, Marian smiled as she scrubbed the plates. They made sure she knew she had to contribute to the festivities, too, leaving her the sticky dishes. "I can't believe they baked me a cake!"

"I'm jealous," said Nancy, drying the dishes beside her. "They never made me one. I think they really appreciated you going to visit Lisa. It was so dangerous for them, and they felt bad that they couldn't."

"I'm glad I could do something useful, anyway. Um, is Lisa okay? She seems to be avoiding me."

"Doug moved back." Nancy said, whispering into her ear.

"Oh no! I should talk to her."

"Everyone already has. Maybe you should wait. She's feeling a bit beaten down. Nobody here thinks she should have allowed him to move in again. She's worried we'll report her and they'll take Billy."

Marian tried to catch Lisa's eye, but she turned away and started packing up her things. Maybe Nancy was right and she should wait to discuss Doug. Meanwhile, she could show all the love she could and try to rebuild her trust.

There was one piece of cake left—the women saved Marian and Nancy a piece to bring home for later, but that left another spare. She wrapped it up in tinfoil, and carried it over to Lisa, catching her at the door. "Here, Lisa—there's a leftover piece. I thought maybe Doug might appreciate your baking. Or you could not tell him and have another piece to enjoy yourself."

Lisa stopped. "It wasn't just me."

"But you helped. Here. We already have our pieces and I really don't need another, tasty though it is!" She patted her stomach, showing the influence of the first year weight gain.

A weak smile flickered on Lisa's face. "Thanks. I'm sure… he'll like it." She tucked it carefully into her diaper bag and pushed the stroller with Billy in it out the door.

Baby steps, thought Marian.

33

Road to Jerusalem

Back at the school, Marian and Albert were suddenly swamped with their courses and projects. They wound up in the library for hours, each at a different end, so they wouldn't be tempted to chat. Albert still didn't talk about what he was working on and Marian felt hurt at his lack of trust.

So she didn't want to ask him about the reincarnation thing, not yet, anyhow. She held her secret inside and focused instead on studying the many many books about Mary. Dr. Rutgers avoided her, darting out of the building when he saw her coming. Why? She had no idea.

She was so busy she missed the protest march after yet another woman was shot by her partner, though she'd vowed to go to any of the demonstrations as part of her desire to work on advocacy. Albert went. Fortunately for Albert, he'd taken command over from Craig and no one got arrested this time. The media was disappointed but covered the story, anyway.

Marian felt guilty letting him down, but she realized she still feared crowds or mobs. She couldn't forget they could so easily go wrong.

* * *

She remembered pushing through the great masses of people when she and Yeshua and his crowds went into Jerusalem that last week. She begged him not to continue. His disciples were getting too loud and angry, and Yeshua kept making demands of the religious leaders. She saw them at the edges of the crowds, eyebrows lowered, rage painted across their faces like graffiti. Sometimes she sensed they were holding stones in their sleeves. The day her son had thrown all of their favourite merchants out of the local Temple, she dragged Yeshua out the back way, afraid they'd kill him right then. Magda helped her pull. She was desperate, carrying Yeshua's child, and so afraid she'd have a baby without a father.

"Mother, you know I have to leave for Jerusalem," Yeshua protested. "My father needs me."

"Your father?" Miryam hesitated. Daniel and Yoseph were long dead. Unless he meant the Father, God, who Yeshua had taken to calling on of late like some crazy person. Like John the Baptist. If he wasn't careful, she warned him, he'd end up just like John, a head shorter. Besides, in Miryam's faith, it was best not to appear too close to God. He could get angry, and His servants, too.

"It's time," Yeshua went on, ignoring her, "Can't you hear them shouting for me? I have to go."

"They are fools and manipulators, Yeshua. You know this. Don't you remember the time with John, when they pulled out your hair? That time they expected you to feed everyone but refused to contribute anything until you shamed them into it?

The time they asked you to wake up poor Lazarus, not letting him rest until he died? They'll either expect you to heal them or lead them into battle. They want to use you. It's not safe!"

Magda wailed, "What about our baby, Yeshua? I'm frightened. I'm afraid they'll hurt us."

Yeshua turned on her then. "I thought you understood," he said, his voice filled with contempt. "I assumed you, at least, had faith. If you doubt me, stay here with my mother. You can be old women together."

Magda clung to him, weeping, until Miryam couldn't stand it any longer.

"Stop it," she said to Magda. "And you, Yeshua, this is no way to speak to your mother and wife. I didn't raise you to be this way. Don't you remember 'bless the meek'?"

He laughed at that, his face softening. He gestured at the two women. "And you call this meek? You terrify me." He hugged them both. "Absolve me, my Marys. The moment overcame me. Thank you for reminding me I am all too humanly fallible."

He still went into the town. Miryam and Magda walked behind him, watching the crowd. Miryam had some of the more sensible followers do the same. The main ones were all silly with their popularity. That cursed Judas, for example, he was at the head of the crowd, drumming up support and shouting anti-Roman protests. Waving palm fronds at everyone, encouraging the crowds to strip the trees and lay palms on the street to mock the Roman processions. One man even found Yeshua a donkey to ride so that everybody could see him better. The donkey was supposed to mock the Roman parade horses. The guards in their shiny armour and rattling on their steeds got the joke. They weren't happy.

Despite this, the parade into town had surprisingly turned

out all right. Everyone seemed happy, except the priests, and there were too many people watching for them to cause any trouble. Miryam was able relax with Magda after they set up camp at Gesthemane. They settled under a shade tree until she overheard the apostles discussing their next plans.

"Did you catch how they loved him? We could easily put together an army, take out the Romans once and for all." Judas sounded over-excited, eager, his voice an octave higher than usual.

"Yeah," said Matthew. "I'm ready to fight." He danced around the cooking fire, wielding a stick. Miryam shuddered. He was a child, playing with toys.

"I can't wait," said Thomas. "Did you see the Centurions making fun of him? I wanted to take them out, right then."

Miryam and Magda gaped at each other in horror. Magda slipped off to fetch Yeshua from their tent.

He listened to them, stood up and stormed into the ring around the fire, livid. "Are you insane?" Yeshua cried. "Haven't you listened to me at all? There will be no fighting. My message has always been of peace. Why do you think they allow us to exist?"

"You weren't very peaceful in the synagogue the other day," said Matthew with a sulk. "That looked an awful lot like fighting to me."

"Yes." Judas walked toward Yeshua. "Do you honestly believe you can win over all these people with words and healing alone? They'll get bored, they always do, and we will lose everything. We need results! Have we wasted all of these months away from our families, recruiting followers? What was it for?"

"I missed the birth of my son," whined Thomas. "My wife left me and returned to her home. I have no family. Yet you bring yours with you." He pointed at Miryam and Magda. Yeshua looked at the women. "They follow me, I do not bring them. They work as hard, nay harder than any of us. Would you wish their hardship on your wives and children?"

The men looked away. They well remembered the reaction of their families when they'd asked them to come along. It hadn't been positive. Thomas' wife had boxed his ears.

"But Yeshua, we've been occupied so long. It's the perfect time to mobilize to evict the Romans. You must admit we have the momentum." Judas stabbed at the fire, sending angry sparks spiralling upwards.

"And how would we expel the Romans? Kill them? They'd come back a hundredfold and crush us."

"Amen," replied Thomas.

"And we'd all wind up in hell together. My father prefers peace. There is too little of it in the world."

"But, Master," Matthew started.

Yeshua swept his arm up, down. "No, no more." He turned away. "I must rest for tomorrow. Get to bed yourselves." He took Magda's hand and left the group.

Miryam moved into the darkness but lingered near the circle. She wished to hear the men.

"What do you expect he has planned for tomorrow? More 'blessed are the poor' stuff? That'll draw a throng." Judas spat into the fire. It hissed.

"Yeah, a flock with rotten fruit. People loathe that speech."

"I think I should speak with Caiaphas. Maybe he'd help us. The high priests hate Rome as much as we do." Judas looked at the others for support.

Matthew frowned. "No. Caiaphas hates Yeshua. He'd give him up in an instant. Probably wouldn't ask for a favour in exchange, either."

"Yeah," Thomas said. "I doubt he'd be an ally. Do they really despise Rome as they pretend? Or are they okay with them being in charge? I haven't heard any anti-Rome preaching in the Temple of late."

Judas kicked a coal back into the fire. "Still," he argued. "He might see the power of a willing crowd of disciples to take on Rome. I'm going to go to him, anyway. Nothing to lose."

Miryam tiptoed away, hoping to warn Yeshua, but when she found him, he was so sound asleep curled in Magda's arms that she didn't have the heart to wake him.

34

Dr. Rutger

When Marian arrived at Compass the next week, she was harried and worried about her project and Albert, who seemed altogether too attached and yet too secretive for her liking. She booked an appointment with Dr. Rutgers to discuss her thesis progress but he was busy with his own book and told her she would have to wait. Meanwhile, the things she read were confusing her more and more. And Albert still wouldn't tell her what he was working on. What was he afraid of? And what was it they were supposed to have in common, other than fear of being really seen?

At the group, she noticed Lisa was still avoiding her. She tried once to get her to answer a question, but only got monosyllables in reply and Lisa quickly found an excuse to move away.

"What's up?" Marian asked one of the other girls.

"Don't know. She not talking to nobody."

They held the meeting, but the women were quiet, uncertain, sensing something wrong. They would speak and glance sideways at Lisa. Or try to pull her into the conversation.

"Billy's getting so big! And look at his smile!"

"Yeah, what do you feed him? My Denzel is so fussy."

Lisa muttered a few sullen words and then carried Billy off to a corner to change him. She took an unusually long time. The women made faces at each other and started to talk amongst themselves. Stories spun between them and laughter covered their unease.

Their babies weren't fooled. They picked up on the tension and acted it out. They fussed and whined and wriggled the whole meeting until everyone was cranky and hot.

As they were cleaning up, Marian whispered to Nancy. "Can't you call someone? She's obviously having a difficult time. She can't sit still."

"Look, if I called every time someone was having a bad day, I'd be on the phone all day, and none of these people would come back." The cross babies were bugging Nancy, too. "It's a fine line between helping and being too controlling. I believe that coming here will give Lisa the strength to do what she has to do herself." She ran her hand through her hair, shoving it behind her ears. "There does seem to be something big happening with the gang. The police are doing hard enforcement lately. Maybe they rounded up some of the guys."

"I hope so," prayed Marian. "Doug, especially."

After another hour of cranky babies and cross mothers, it was time to go. As the women loaded up their screaming babies, Nancy pulled her aside. "I found out what's going on. Lisa has moved to a shelter."

"Oh, my God! Is she going to be okay? What can we do?"

"You saw her today. She's a mess. I think she's hoping for housing soon, in a different neighbourhood. I just hope she can come to Compass."

* * *

Depressed after her morning, she wandered to Dr. Rutger's office, hoping to catch him in a quiet moment. There was a new professor sitting at his desk, a young, balding, extremely serious-looking priest in a collar.

Marian poked her head in the door. "Where's Dr. Rutgers?"

"Who? Oh, the previous professor? He… had to go on leave rather suddenly."

"Oh, no—he's not sick, is he?"

The priest coughed delicately behind his hand. "He's fine. He just needed some time off. Now, why were you looking for him?"

"I was hoping for some guidance about my term project," said Marian, "but I guess I'll have to wait until he gets back."

"No, no, no," the priest replied. "No need for that. I'm covering his classes and supervisions. I'll help you."

"Do you know what I am working on?"

"Yes, yes, I've been briefed." He stood, put out his hand to shake. It was warm and the slightest bit moist. "I'm Dr. Handspiker. I'll be covering for the foreseeable future. Now, let's have a look at your proposal. Please sit, Ms.…."

"Steeves, Marian Steeves."

"Ah." The priest shuffled through a heap of papers on the desk, found her proposal. He pulled it out of the pile, tsking as the rest tumbled to the floor.

Marian tidied up the stack and replaced it, then sat. She pulled at the thread on her thrift store scarf while she watched him read. She had undone several inches by the time he spoke.

His voice had gone all high-pitched. "Well, this is quite something. I'll want to review some of these assertions. You'll need serious references for most of what you've suggested— some of it sounds blasphemous, even. The Son of God conceived by a man? His speeches coming from lessons Mary taught him as a child?" He sounded grave. "I don't see it getting past the committee."

"Dr. Rutgers told me he already had it cleared."

Dr. Handspiker shook his head, slowly, backward and forward. "I'm not sure how much of Rutgers' approvals will carry, Ms. Steeves. He has been... is being... somewhat discredited here at the college. Something about his presentation on Peter. He had the gall to present blasphemy to the Bishop!"

Marian felt sweat forming behind her ears. "But he is a tenured prof! And he already gave me the go-ahead!"

"Yes, yes, that may be so, but he's obviously not well. He collapsed after his statement, and he is in the hospital."

"What? Can we go visit him? Is he going to recover?"

"I don't believe so, Marian. I shouldn't be telling you this but he seems to have had a stroke. He cannot speak and they feel it will only be days until he is summoned heavenward, though with that last mumbo-jumbo, his destination may have changed." He hummed and fussed with his shirt. "Be that as it may, we had to race over and give him Extreme Unction and now we wait. We have one of our nuns sitting with him, praying he will recant. Strange thing— we received a written Urbi and Orbi concerning him from the Pope this morning." The priest crossed himself. "I have never seen such a blessing before. Particularly a faxed one!" He made a face. "I suppose we will have to hold a grand funeral mass, and they will repeat his sacrilege. The Eastern Orthodox people have already offered to host. More noise, signifying nothing, I fear."

Marian froze. "That is bizarre," she agreed. "He taught us it was an exceedingly rare thing." Marian wondered if all of this was because of Peter's revelation. Would he be finished reincarnating? Would he at last be free? Why? Could she?

"I've got to see him," she said. "Which hospital is he in?"

"I don't know that they are allowing visitors."

"Please! It's urgent. He asked me something... I need to give him my answer. Please?"

Dr. Handspiker stared at Marian for a moment, then took a pen and paper out of his desk and wrote a number on it, signed it. "This note will let you in to see him. Please do not share this with your classmates. He really is very ill, and too much bother could make him suffer. And who knows what additional heresy he may spread in his illness?"

"Thank you so much! I will tiptoe in as quiet as I can and try not to unsettle him—I just want to say goodbye."

35

Reincarnation

Marian couldn't stop shivering. She wasn't certain what was happening, wasn't sure what it meant for her, for Peter, for their endless reincarnations. She had to ask Peter what it was all about. Without speaking to anyone else, she slipped off campus and race-walked to the hospital. Peter was also in the grim place that Lisa had recovered in, but a different wing. It took her an unconscionably long time to find the room, and the entire time she was breathing fast, pulse racing, trembling.

The door was shut when she reached his room. No, she thought, he can't be gone yet? She dreaded being left alone to figure everything out. Gently, she pushed open the door, spotted the sheet-draped feet at the end of the bed. She tiptoed in, staring at the sheet as she scanned up his body, hoping that it wasn't pulled over his face or anything.

"Hello."

Marian jumped out of her skin and was just settling to the ground when she turned her head and saw a bland-faced nun in her early eighties. She was sitting on a chair beside the wall, holding her rosary in one hand and Dr. Rutger's hand in the other. She looked exceedingly calm.

Marian did not. "Whoa. You startled me!" She tried to tuck in her scarf and look a bit less like a windstorm.

"I apologize. He hasn't had many visitors, so I wasn't expecting anyone." She laughed gently. "You scared me, too!"

Marian held out the note from Professor Handspiker. It was damp from her sweating as she ran. "I'm so sorry. Dr. Rutgers was my thesis advisor. I felt terrible when I heard how sick he was. I knew I had to come and see him, before…"

"Yes, yes," the sister said. "I know the befores." She waved away the paper. "Would you like to have a moment or two alone with him? He wakes up every once in a while. I could use a break, to be honest."

"Thank you," Miriam said. "I'll let the nurses know if anything happens."

"There's no need of that, dear. He is ready to move on. We are just waiting for the moment."

Maria switched places with the nun, taking the warm seat. The nun shook her rosary towards Marian. "Do you need these?"

"No, thanks." That would be strange, praying to herself, Marian wondered. The thought made her squeamish. She usually skipped those prayers at church.

The sister nodded and glided soundlessly out of the room. The door whispered shut.

Suddenly, Dr. Rutger's hand grabbed Marian's. Holding back her scream, she looked back at him.

"Get that woman out of here!" he puffed out between tortured breaths. One side of his mouth couldn't keep up and hung, inert. A dribble of saliva hung in the corner.

Marian pulled a tissue out of the tiny hospital box and wiped the dribble away before thinking. He made a face. "Sorry for the invasion of space." She tucked the tissue into the overflowing bag beside the bed. She gazed at him, tears starting in her eyes. She dashed them away. "Are you in pain? Can I get you anything? Are you sure you want her gone? She seems very nice."

He shook his head no. "Damn… woman keeps… praying… over me. It's depressing." He gave her a lopsided smile. "Glad to… see you. Think I may have…" He paused, closed his eyes.

Marian held her breath. Would he speak again?

"Done it." he added.

"What?" Marian asked, holding his hand firmly. "Done what?"

"Finished… it." He lay back, breathing heavily. "Wanted to… let… you know it could… be done. Just… needed to be a bit brave…"

"Brave, how? What did you do? Are you sure? What happened?"

He didn't answer, shutting his eyes in a way that seemed final.

Dr. Rutgers lay quiet now, except for his ragged breathing. As Marian sat, transfixed, wondering, his breaths started the death pattern she knew so well. Shallow breaths building up to a big breath, then getting more shallow until breathing stopped for a minute. Marian waited. The next gasp of breath startled many, but she was waiting for it as he inhaled deeply. The breathing pattern was heartrending, but familiar. Families would endure as their loved one seemed to have passed, only to have them gulp in another unexpected breath. The space after the breaths would gradually get longer until it spun out into eternity.

Into eternity? Marian sat back, dizzy. Had he finished it? Was he no longer reincarnating? How had he managed that? She watched closely as he slipped away, seeking some sign of his soul escaping, some brightness as he was taken to heaven, if there was one. She didn't see any change, small or large, that she hadn't seen in the many other people she'd sat beside as they died. Perhaps that was the point? Her head ached as she stood up, wrapped her coat around herself, ready to leave once the nun came back.

She wondered how she could manage the same escape. He seemed so quiet, so calm. Content. She watched him until she was sure he was gone, then offered a silent prayer. Looking at Peter's inert form, she couldn't help a prayer for herself, too. "Not yet, okay, God? Not quite yet."

The nun tiptoed back into the room, holding a cup of tea. "Thanks, I needed that break." She stepped next to the bed. "But he's gone! His spirit has left." Without warning, the nun burst into sobs, her body moving forward and backward like a wave.

"Are you all right?" Marian asked her, feeling stupid. Obviously the nun was not okay. She helped her into the chair, wrapped a blanket around her. The nun resisted, pushed her away.

"Leave us alone! Please!" The nun waved a sodden handkerchief at Marian. "Go. He's not here, anyway. There's no need for you to stay. Go, now!"

Marian, slightly insulted, pulled open the door and stepped into the noisy hallway. A nurse was racing by and she stopped her, told her that the patient in room 415 was dead. That Peter was dead.

The nurse nodded. "Oh, I'm glad. It wasn't a long time for him."

Marian sniffed back tears. "The nun in there seems to be really upset."

"She's probably a family member. I'll look after her once I give this med to the patient next door. Thanks for letting me know." She sped off down the hallway, needle in hand.

Marian thought of going back in, to check on the nun, but her head was shooting electric sparks of possibilities and she couldn't quite get into the grief mode. After all, Peter was free, wasn't he? It's not like he hadn't died before.

36

So Much For That

The exuberance about her possible liberation lasted until Marian got back to the residence and found a message from Dr. Handspiker, demanding she see him immediately.

She raced over to his office, feeling scattered and confused. Dr. Handspiker's scowl didn't help. He gestured with one swift hack of his hand for her to sit down, and instantly started tearing apart her thesis proposal, line by line. He had underlined everything that appeared the slightest bit controversial. In bright red. "Consider deleting this here. And this. And this is heresy. Take it out." The scratching of ballpoint on paper seemed interminable. "Where did you hear this? Are you kidding me?" He kept making surreptitious signs of the cross as if he feared her paper's content. "You realize this is a dangerous downward spiral. Follow your thoughts and the entire story falls apart. It is positively evil."

Marian listened without answering, perspired, and managed to thank him. She gathered up her papers and wobbled out of the office, awash in worry. What would she do now, now that he cast her proposal into the gaping maw of hellfire? But she knew her information to be true! How would she prove it? Why was Dr. Handspiker so agitated?

Never mind, she told herself. She'd work harder, get references, take out what she could not confirm, still try to put some flesh on Miryam's sainted bones. If nothing else, she'd have the satisfaction of finding out everything she could about herself. Figure out why she kept reincarnating. Maybe even decipher how Peter escaped, if he had. And if the priest didn't like it, she'd find another advisor. Surely someone in the college had a slightly open mind.

She headed for the university archives, looking for the resources and books in their original language. The university didn't have a huge selection, but few people bothered to refer to them, so she could usually find what she wanted. The university also had made copies of some older documents from other universities back when they still had money for libraries. She hadn't explored all of those yet.

She wondered if they had any records of other Urbi and Orbi declarations about people. She didn't remember hearing of any. Could this mean Peter was decisively on the road to beatification? They'd been calling him a saint for centuries, but he'd been here. Did this mean the other saints weren't really saints? Surely Peter would be one of the first. She was so confused.

Marian had carefully omitted her language ability when she applied to AST—thought it would make her seem freakish— but the perpetual reincarnation somehow left fragments of languages behind in her head. With a little practice she had brushed up her Aramaic and Greek and could use it now to read through the documents in their original formats. After an hour of reading, she leaned back, smiling. It was a revelation. There were women here.

37

Revelations

The next week she was down in the stacks, reading the Gospel of Pseudo-Matthew, when she noticed Albert head down in a book a few carrels down. They'd stopped speaking much, not broken up, exactly, just acting cooler as the days lengthened. They hadn't made it to girlfriend-boyfriend, but Marian missed the closeness and the warmth of being cared for and caring for. Maybe he was tired of waiting for her to be more present?

Surely he'd understand her skittishness. He knew she'd had a letter from Neil last week via one of her New Brunswick friends and it had sent her into a tailspin. He was apparently still quite angry. She'd turned off her cell phone, afraid of being located, spent the week hiding in her dorm room, afraid to go out. If Neil thought she had a male friend, there's no telling what he'd do. Surely Albert understood all that?

Maybe he was just distant. He seemed terribly busy all of a sudden, working on courses and his project and helping with the protesters. He returned silent and thoughtful after his sessions with them, almost disturbed. Was he planning to be a minister after all and decided she wasn't a good choice for a partner? Or was he mad she didn't go with him to the protests? Marian missed him.

She walked by his carrel, casually looking at the desk as she touched his shoulder. He slammed the book shut but not before she saw that it was in Latin.

"You know Latin? A fisherman's boy like you? Cool!"

"You read Aramaic?"

Marian reeled. "Sneak!"

"Cheater, cheater. No wonder you did so well in Dr. R's class."

They glared at one another for a moment. Then Albert spun around and stood up, blocking Marian's escape. "When were you going to tell me?"

"How long have you known?" she asked.

"It's easy to figure out. You keep signing out those books. I can never get the Aramaic ones. You always have them."

"What about you? Learn Latin at school? And where'd you pick up Aramaic?"

"School, or something like that." Albert hugged her, quickly, and pulled over a chair for her. "Look, since you caught me out, I'll tell you what you want to know. My project is about Jesus's father. So there."

"Which one?"

"The 'angel,' silly. Joseph doesn't count and God's already covered."

"There was another? Well, aren't you the rebel! Have you run it by your adviser yet? Dr. R's replacement just slammed me for my topic. I dislike him intensely."

"I gave her the rough outlines. I didn't want to show my cards until I have some proof of what I think."

"Which is what?"

"I'm examining if JC had a human father. I'm not sure why. It seems like a lot of the birth story matches the Old Testament too closely. What if they just made it up to match things? Doesn't it all seem a bit Zeus-y?"

"It does. But that doesn't mean it isn't true," Marian said. "Anyway, it's so cute you are doing Jesus's dad since I'm doing his mum. It's like we planned it." She wagged jazz hands at him.

"Yeah. That's why I didn't tell you. I thought you'd figure I was copying you or trying to ride on your studies. Or the profs would get cross."

"I know—you were just flirting."

Albert grinned. "Well, yes, that too. Were we fighting? I forget. What was it about?"

She smiled at him. "I can't remember, either. I'm sure it was about nothing important. But you're not getting away that easily. Where did you learn the languages? It's almost impossible to find anyone who teaches them nowadays."

"I can read Hebrew, too. Maybe I'm good at languages? I like to study?"

"Not good enough. Hey, Dr. R. kept advising me to get together with you, that we had a lot in common. What do you suppose he meant by that?"

"Well, now we see we have the languages in common. That's gotta mean something."

"Again, how? Seriously, Albert, where did you pick up those languages? I'm positive they didn't show up on your local school curriculum. And didn't you do biology for undergrad?"

"Could ask you the same question."

They looked at each other again, blocked. Moments passed.

Albert looked down, sideways, up. He scratched the hair on his arm. "Well," he drawled finally, "they do use Latin words in biology. All the names are in Latin."

Marian shook her head. "But you were studying full sentences—of old Latin even. And you say you read Aramaic?"

"Only some words."

"But how? And that can't be the only reason Dr. R. seemed so interested in you."

"He was? That's weird. I've barely spoken two words to him all year. He knows nothing about me."

She stood up, frustration creasing her face. "Come on. Why are we dancing around each other? Do you have the same weird things happening to you as I do? How?"

"You'll think I am crazy. And hey, you know way more of this stuff than I do. It's as if you were there."

Marian stepped back. "What a ridiculous suggestion. Do I look 2000 years old?"

Albert snorted. "If I say yes, will you still speak to me? I mean, you are looking a wee bit tired."

"Oh, ha ha. Something's fishy. Have you been following me?"

"Um, no. I've been walking right beside you. I've even been sleeping beside you now and again. If you let me, I'd be doing more than that."

"Okay, quick quiz. What's an appropriate name from Jesus's time?"

"Um, I don't recall. Say Miryam?"

"That was easy. Another."

"What about Daniel?"

Marian leaned forward, placed her hands on each side of Albert's head, pulled him toward her.

"Ow! What are you doing? That hurts!"

Marian held tight, peered into Albert's eyes. "Are you in there?"

"Ummm, yes?"

"What do you think of the Judean rebellion?"

"Killed without trial. Evil Romans."

"How were they executed?"

"Look, we've studied all this stuff…"

"Okay," said Marian. "How did the Judeans get food and clothing when they lived in the hills? Just before the Romans wiped them out?"

"I gathered somewhere there was this sweet girl who delivered food every day and fixed their clothes by the fire."

"Why would she risk that? She'd have been stoned!" Marian was quivering now, unable to contain her excitement.

"Well, we caught her hanging out with a Roman and she didn't want us to tell."

"We?" Marian let go of Albert's face, collapsed back onto her chair. "You're surely not telling me that you remember being there?"

"Nuts, isn't it? But I feel as if I were. It's probably just a dream. Or a movie I've half-forgotten."

"Or a life you've half-forgotten. Do you have any more of these 'dreams'?"

"Oh yeah, tons. I used to assume they were because of bad weed, but I don't partake any more. I see people living on mountains, by a huge lake, on the Russian tundra in the freezing winter… and I constantly seem to be a part of the story. Think I'm losing it? I find them springing up everywhere these days. The last time we had wine with dinner—did you notice I was an awfully long time in the bathroom?"

"Yeah! I wondered about that. I thought you'd come down

with Norwalk again, but you were all wired when you came back."

"I had flipped into some memory or another. But it can't be real. I mean, I've never been to Spain. Was scary as heck—we were being chased by the police. There was some kind of war going on. I tried to pull myself out of the dream but I couldn't right away. It terrified me. I must have had some kind of fever. After we got home, I almost checked myself into student health but then I remembered that they'd probably send me for assessment at that creepy hospital your friend frequents, so I decided to ignore it and focus on you. Maybe it would go away, right?"

Marian laughed, shakily. "You are a man, aren't you?" She took a deep breath. "Would it help your mental health if I told you I have the same thing happen to me, all the time?"

"Weird. It explains the burnt toast, though. You always seem to forget what you are doing. I wonder if there's something in the air ducts or maybe our water? What if we are going insane?"

Marian sighed. "What if we've actually lived all those lives, and just keep reincarnating into new ones?"

Albert gaped at her. "Are you a secret Buddhist? Is this why you keep asking me about reincarnation all the time? Maybe you are the thing messing with my head."

"Geez. I asked about that twice. Twice. Look, let's skip it for now. Do you need me to describe some of the older readings for you? Is there any language you don't know?"

"Show-off. I'm not sure if you are safe anymore."

"I'm more safe than you appreciate. Just trust me." Marian hugged him, held his body shape in her arms, speculated. Could this be her Daniel?

Albert smiled back, but pulled out of her arms. "Whatevs, as they say. Hey, how about we head out for supper and pretend we've never heard of Christianity? I'm about ready to swear to atheism, myself."

"Me, too. Besides, I'm starving. Should we get some fish and chips? I must have some grease."

38

Finding

They grabbed a bus and hopped on the harbour ferry across to Dartmouth, for the chance to breathe sea air and gaze at the lights and the huge seagoing vessels. Once the ferry docked, they race-walked up the hill to their favourite fish and chips place, John's Diner, where everything was cooked with real gobs of fat, and arrived hot and tasty and totally artery-destroying.

They sat in the booth by the stained photo of the once-visiting Adrienne Clarkson and John Ralston Saul, hoping for inspiration.

Marian tried to talk, couldn't, then blurted, "So give. What's your history that you know all that stuff?"

Albert frowned. "Remember, I could ask you the very same thing. I'll bet Moncton doesn't have a Latin curriculum either."

Marian reached across the table, held Albert's hands tight. "Promise you won't have me committed," she asked, just as Albert burst out,

"I know I told you they were dreams, but…"

They said, "What?" simultaneously.

"Are you telling me that we both have been doing this reincarnation thing?" Marian pushed her fish and chips to the side, forgot them.

Albert looked down. Shrugged. "Since way back around the time around Jesus, yeah," he mumbled.

"Oh my God!"

"Exactly. I figure whatever God is must've had something to do with this."

"So, who were you, at the beginning I mean." Marian couldn't wait to hear if she'd been right, that her Daniel was right there, in front of her.

"I was pretty much the same—a guy who went with a crowd and protested once too often."

"Where? Where?" Marian's voice was raising, but she didn't care. The restaurant was always deafeningly loud. Pans crashed together in the background.

"I think I was in Judea. I remember some hills and things. And the Romans."

"And your NAME was?" Marian almost yelled.

"Oh, I was Daniel, I think, like in the lion's den. Who were you?"

Marian, folded onto the table, getting tartar sauce on her hair. She felt queasy, unreal, freaked out. She couldn't meet his eyes until her head raised despite herself. Albert was staring at her, his pupils dilated.

"It can't be," he gasped.

"It is…" she said. "Miryam."

"Miryam!" Albert grabbed her arms in a way that felt almost desperate. "I never had time to say goodbye—I'm so sorry. I've missed you for so long!"

"I cried for days," Marian said. "My mother slapped me. And

when she found out I was pregnant..."

"You were pregnant? With... our... child?"

"Yes. And you'll never guess who he turned out to be."

Words tumbled out, all the words they hadn't said for centuries, tales of love and disbelief and shared goals and happiness and hopes. Stories of the world and what happened where, where they'd each been at certain times. It seemed they'd crossed paths before. In Bosnia. In Africa. In Mexico. Somehow they hadn't made the connection. In Mexico, Daniel had had a crush on Maria, but she ran off and married Antonio. It depressed him for months after that, like he'd let someone down.

By the end of the meal, they were holding greasy hands and not minding a bit.

"Marry me for real?" Albert asked. He froze, shocked that he actually asked the question. "I mean..."

Marian smiled, then turned her face away for a moment. "No," she said. "Last time I married you, you got killed. I'm not risking that again." She pointed upwards. "I don't want to make anyone mad at us." Everyone I love dies or gets murdered or kills me, she thought. Which would happen with Albert? She looked at his dejected expression, stroked his hand. "I'll live with you, though, if that's okay. You know I love you. Forever. And ever."

Albert grinned, sagged, relieved. "Well, if you insist. I might keep asking, though. Fair warning. And hey, remember, living in sin is still a problem in some circles. I wonder if our old 'marriage' still holds?" He leaned across the table and kissed her, hard. She responded until they were stopped by the wave of applause that filled the small diner.

39

Doug Returns

Marian floated into Compass the next day. Albert had spent the night, and it was wonderful, even better than when they were lying together in the tent in Judea. Now that she had found her Daniel, she seemed to be more comfortable in her body, like it fit better or something, or the lumps and bumps from her previous lives were being ironed out.

The women noticed her glow and teased her about it, winking at her and each other. "Someone got some, I'm thinking," said one, and laughter rolled across the group. Marian wondered how they knew, but she saw her face when she fled into the bathroom and she could tell from the glow. Well, that and the almost-hickey that wasn't quite hidden on her neck. They'd been a bit over-enthusiastic.

The women were all sitting around the table for their snack when the door banged open, rattling the windows.

"Lisa!" a voice roared. Three babies immediately started screaming. Their mothers raced over to pick them up.

Lisa froze. Marian, without thinking, stood up in front of

her, arms out, blocking her from the door and Doug. Nancy slipped silently backward into the kitchen she'd just left with a tray of black bean brownies.

Doug thundered into the room, waving a knife, one of those big ones from Canadian Tire, the kind you can skin a moose with. The smell of booze preceded him, and his pupils were widely dilated. He swung the blade around, weaving back and forth, scanning.

Marian shuddered. That knife! She could almost feel it slicing into her skin. She backed in closer to Lisa, pushing her slowly away from Doug.

The other women slid their chairs back, grabbed their babies, moved away from the table towards the back wall. They screamed and yelled until Doug waved the knife their way. Lisa pushed Billy under the table with one foot. She'd strapped him in his chair for his nap, but he was awake now. He didn't cry, just looked. It seemed like he'd seen this happen before.

One woman slid her cell out of her pocket, palming it in under her baby, trying to call for help. She wasn't fast enough. "No phones," Doug shouted. "Drop them. All of you." He leaned toward the women again, waving the knife.

The women carefully placed their phones on the table and stepped back. They didn't want him to break them.

"You too, Lisa," Doug yelled. "Give me your damn phone!" Lisa put hers on the floor, kicked it over towards him. "What the fuck did you do? Bitch! You moved. Where the hell did you go? If you think I'm going to let you keep me away from my goddamned kid, you're more stupid than you look."

He strutted up towards Marian. She braced herself, but she wasn't prepared as he stepped quickly to the side and hip-checked her into the table. She cracked her skull and fell to the floor, wrenching her neck and landing painfully on her shoulder. Doug was inches away from Lisa now, the knife pointed straight at her stomach. Marian tried to kick him away with her foot and got a kick in return for her trouble. She tried again, stood, and pushed him away from Lisa with all her strength. Doug turned, flicked his knife. Marian felt warm oozing on her abdomen. Enraged, she attacked him again, but Doug focused on Lisa, shoving the knife forward. Lisa leaned away, but he grabbed her, pulling the knife and Lisa together.

"No," one woman shouted. "You hurt her enough!" She put her baby down and ran at Doug, flailing her arms. The other mothers looked at her, and each other, and did the same. Within moments, women surrounded Doug, pummelling him with their fists. They shoved him away from Lisa. They punched his back, slapped his face, thumped him. One mum swung her baby car seat through the air, trying to connect with Doug's head.

He still had the knife and was swinging it around, but the women had arranged themselves like a pack of wolves. When he'd turn his back on one of them, that one would attack him, scratching him with her nails and punching and kicking him. He'd spin back and the women on the other side would take their turn. The car seat flew in circles, connected once. Doug wobbled. The women cheered and renewed their attack.

Lisa stood straight, not trying to move away. Marian looked at her, wondering why, when she spotted the blood seeping from Lisa's side. She slid forward, just in time to catch her as Lisa fainted, crumpling to the ground.

"No, no, no," Marian wailed. "Not again…" She held Lisa tight, trying to press her hand against the wound.

The women continued their battle, some of them cut now,

blood splattering everywhere. So many injuries were on their arms and hands, Marian saw. Defensive wounds. They fought well. At one point, Doug glanced over at Lisa and saw her flat on the floor. He paled, and whirled around, racing for the exit.

The women chased him, right into the arms of four angry Halifax policemen, who knocked him down and added their own kicks into the mix. For once, no one took phone pictures of police brutality.

40

Wounds and Healing

Nancy ran back into the room and hurried to Lisa. "The ambulance is coming—how is she doing?"

"Not great. She's passed out."

Nancy pulled some receiving blankets from the donation pile and threw them to Marian. "Try pressing with these." She turned to the other women. "How many of you guys are hurt?"

They gawked, uncomprehending. They were still high from battle. Gradually they looked at each other, saw the cuts and blood everywhere. The babies screamed. It was a shrieking melee, women running to get their babies and then, realizing they were bleeding everywhere, dashing back to the sink to wash off.

Nancy took charge of them, getting them lined up, the cleanest ones to look after the babies first, while she tried to stop some of the bleeding in the others.

Meanwhile, Marian put Lisa's legs up on a chair and laid her flat. She didn't dare release the fist pressed hard on Lisa's wound for more than a second as the women brought her more and more blankets. She hoped the pressure she was applying would help slow the blood. Looking down she saw she, too was turning red with her own blood, flowing slower than Lisa's but still present. She took one of the receiving blankets and pressed it against her stomach with her other hand.

An ambulance screamed around the corner and parked and the room filled with more people in uniforms. Lisa was whisked off as soon as they'd put in an IV. Another ambulance arrived, full of paramedics, who patched up the other women and took the other, more badly injured to the hospital.

The paramedics circled Marian, trying to get her to get in the ambulance with the others. Marian shook her head and said she was fine, that she needed to stay. The cut in her midsection wasn't deep, and they'd bandaged it tightly. Her head had a huge bruise forming, but for now, she felt okay. The paramedics weren't convinced, especially when she tried to walk and wobbled, but when Nancy told them she would go with her to the ER soon for assessment, they didn't insist on taking her. Marian wanted to stay with the women. Her women.

"How'd you call the ambulance?" Marian asked Nancy.

Nancy waggled her phone. "I dialled a quick 911 in after I went into the kitchen. Thank God I could. He was high as a kite. He would have killed her." She jiggled Billy on her lap. "I hope she's okay."

Marian whispered back, "I hope so, too. The paramedics seemed relatively calm. That could be good news, or …"

Marian swallowed and looked around the room. The others sat, shocked and furious, cuddling anxious babies. The anger rose off them like steam.

"Doug blew it now, man."

"Yeah, my man will get him good. Look what he did to my

arm! That's going to scar."

"He cut my fucking tattoo. I paid a lot for that."

"Yeah, but now it's going to look really bad ass."

The women laughed, suddenly, crazily falling on each other, hugging each other, slapping each other on the back. They grabbed Marian and Nancy and pulled them into the crowd, sharing hugs and fist bumps.

"We taught him a lesson!"

"We sure did!"

"You were awesome, Marian! You blocked him like a hockey player! She woulda died, otherwise."

"Go Marian! Go Nancy!"

"You were amazing!" Marian shouted over the yelling.

"We rule!" The women pulled her in again, jumping up and down in a circle.

Everyone cheered. The police stared, slack-jawed, but Marian could see a few smiles among them. Nancy brought out the long-forgotten and usually loathed black bean brownies and they all, women and cops, actually ate them, between laughing and bragging and crying all in turns. Eating and talking—the cure for all ills, thought Marian.

41

Eating and Talking

Marian remembered the time after her son's crucifixion was full of eating and talking. Miryam thought she'd never smile or laugh again. Preparing meals kept her hands busy and her mind quiet.

She kept seeing Yeshua on the cross, the small, pitiful group of women there to witness. She again felt her heart crumbling as she remembered them sitting there that day, mute. Magda made the only noise, a soft sobbing that was even more wrenching for its quiet.

Then Yeshua started his mad death-talk, calling to God, shouting blame. That was worse. Her heart broke when he acknowledged her as she sat there. She was so glad when it was finally over.

Pesky John kept coming by, trying to take the women away. As if she'd abandon her son now, at the end. They'd already forced them apart once, when they were trying to keep Miryam and Magda safe from the crowds, and look at how that worked out.

Judas, with his foolish trusting of the priests, leading them to

Yeshua, thinking they were going to make a pact and act against Rome. Ambition! That had killed her son—his ambition, Judas' ambition, the priest's ambition.

What galled Miryam most was that no one in the end fought for Yeshua. All these men, so ready to let Yeshua lead them against the Roman might, dissolved when faced with actual swords. Peter said Yeshua told them to stop, but Miryam knew that Yeshua had already been dragged away and the skirmish was between the men and the Temple guards. Instead of fighting, they'd seized the women and locked them into a nearby house, with Matthew standing guard, to keep them from following Yeshua. "It's for your safety," they said, but Miryam knew it was because they themselves were afraid.

So she would not leave him now, as he hung on the cross, as they lifted him down, broken and dead. A kind stranger paid for Yeshua's body and she and Magda and the other women took him away, washing away his blood and dressing his body for burial before placing him in the donated tomb. It was a far grander tomb than she'd expected for her son. She tried to repay the kind man, but he refused, and ran away, hastening to be home for the Sabbath and safe.

She'd returned to the men's house then, the other women trailing along. Peter came back and sat in a corner by himself, weeping. There was no sign of Judas, thank god, or Miryam might have had something to say about it. As would the mumbling men. It would be best all around if Judas never showed his face again. The wives, as usual, prepared dinner, such that it was. Bread, some wine, a bit of dried fish.

"Do you remember last night, when we were so happy?" Thomas said.

"Yes, he was happy, too, joking with us."

"Well, but then he got all serious, remember? He kept on about remembering him. It was like he knew."

Magda sobbed once, deeply. Peter reached over to comfort her but she pushed him away. "And where were you when he needed you, Peter? He was looking for you. He called for you. You weren't there."

"I couldn't watch. My heart was breaking. Wasn't yours?" Peter shrilled at her.

"Your courage was broken," Magda shouted back. "Like all the rest of you, too timid to show your faces. Too afraid to stand up for him. You are fakes, frauds..." She collapsed, weeping.

"Be quiet!" Miryam had stormed into the room. They dropped silent in shock. They rarely heard Miryam raise her voice. "Is this how you plan to honour my son's memory? Fighting and yelling?" Silence. "Well, then let's sort out how he wanted to be remembered, and share it as he would have wanted. Let's make sure this tragedy wasn't in vain. We loved him. Now we must share him."

* * *

Miryam dried her hands. "It's Passover, everybody is busy. We must use this time to get his message straight, then go out and continue his work. We will go everywhere, speak to the poor, the rich, talk about peace, the need to love one another. Let people know the old God is gone and our new covenant is with the God Yeshua talked about."

The men cheered. The women smiled. Even Miryam felt uplifted. Her son had died, but she could make sure he was remembered, through his message and his messengers, male and female.

Magda spoke. "What shall I do?"

"You'll come with me," Miryam said. "We have to protect your baby, Yeshua's son. There will be many wanting to hurt him, I fear. Perhaps we should go to one of the mountain villages, remain safe and hidden. The rest of you can come there for a safe place, too. We'll meet, discuss the message and how best to spread news of my son."

"What about his body? It seems wrong to leave him here, not amongst his kin."

"I am more afraid they will use it as a symbol of their hatred. We need to move him, and tonight, while everyone is busy with the Sabbath."

The room rumbled in alarm. "Move him?"

"On the Sabbath? It's forbidden…"

"Where?"

"If they spot us, they'll crucify us, too!"

Miryam looked at them, her eyes accusing. She pointed at Peter and Matthew. "You two, go get his body and put it where the other poor crucified souls rest."

They gasped. Magda sobbed anew.

"No, listen to me, listen! It will be much better this way. If people come to collect his body to defile it, it won't be there. And I know my Yeshua would prefer to be buried with the common people than set aside as better than they are. The Romans have crucified so many of our people for meaningless crimes. He spoke often of his sorrow about their torment. This way, when the world ends, they can all rise to heaven together."

They still looked sceptical, scuffing their feet like little boys. Matthew's lower lip jutted out. Miryam fought an urge to slap him.

She continued, more firmly. "Besides, I would never wish hurt on the kind man who bought my son's body and opened his tomb. And yet he may well be harmed if he is accused and they find Yeshua's body there. He broke many Pharisee rules. If the body isn't there, they cannot punish him."

Finally, they agreed with her logic and left on their errand. The bodies in the crucifixion site were not dressed, so they removed Yeshua's wrappings and laid them, neatly folded in the tomb, marked as they were from his anointing.

42

At Last, Rest

Marian came to herself with a start. Nancy was shaking her shoulder. "Are you okay, Marian?"

"What? Oh…yes. It must be the shock."

"Not surprising. I'm still shivering. And that bump on your head is still growing. Let's get you to the ER. There's nothing more to do here. The police are still investigating and they want us out. I'll tell them to call us if they hear anything about Lisa. Social Services even came and picked up Billy. You were out for a while."

Nancy drove Marian to the hospital, where she sat for some time until she was sutured up and examined for concussion and neck injuries. They X-rayed her and gave her pain medications and called her a cab. When Marian arrived back at the residence, Albert took one look at her face and held her tightly for a very long time. Then he wrapped her in a blanket, sat her on the sofa, and made her a cup of very strong sweet tea.

"Thanks. Whew. Are you trying to keep me wide awake for some reason?"

"Read somewhere that tea was good for shock," Albert said.

"Let me have a sip." He tugged at the cup, took a long drink. Passing it back to her, he said, "I heard about the attack on Twitter. It was horrible. I was scared for you when I saw all those ambulances. I tried to find out where you were but you weren't answering your phone. And there are all these hospitals here. I was just working my way through them when you came in. No one told me anything."

"I didn't have my phone with me. No idea where it went. I was terrified, to be honest. But those women—they were amazing. They came together, took on Doug. He had a knife… he stabbed Lisa before I could stop him… he threw me aside like I was nothing." She started shaking violently. Albert pulled her in to his chest, hugged her until she calmed.

"The police got there just in time. He would have won the fight. But the women were punching him and kicking him, and they kept dancing around him. I hope Lisa's all right." Marian's thoughts were all over the place, skittering like mice.

Albert stroked her hair to quiet her. "Last report said all the injuries were non-life threatening."

"Thank God. And Nancy—wow, she was so fast. She'd slipped out to call the police before he even registered she was there. Amazing. What a group of fantastic women."

"I think you're forgetting someone."

"Who? Me? I was useless. I thought I'd be all protective and stand in front of Lisa but the jerk pushed me down with one shove. Banged my head. Hurt my shoulder. Then he cut me, and I was even more useless."

"Useless doesn't sound at all like you. I bet you're not telling me everything. And wow, you really hurt your head! Look at that bruise!" Albert kissed it, very gently. "Better?"

"Much," she said dryly. "Or maybe it's all the drugs they gave me?"

He pulled her close again and started stroking her hair, gently, over and over. It was so soothing. Then he moved to stroking her arms, from the shoulder down to his fingers, so gently she could only feel his warmth. She dozed. She felt safe.

A memory tugged at her mind, keeping her from sleeping. A moonlit path, the touch of a young man, so long ago. "Daniel?" she mumbled.

"Shh," he said. "Rest."

43

And Found

The next morning, Albert and Marian woke, clasped in each other's arms. Albert stayed the night to be sure that Marian could still wake up. He woke her at regular intervals and checked her eyes until they were both exhausted. Finally, dawn broke, and they gave up on sleep. Albert got up and disappeared, only to come back from the kitchen with steaming mugs of tea. With milk.

"I found fresh milk! Who knew? Milky tea for the shock this time," he said. He sat on the bed and handed the mug to Marian. "Are you up to going to class today? I hope you plan to stay home."

Marian yawned and stretched, wincing when she stretched her neck and shoulder. "I might take today off. I feel like I've been run over by a truck."

"Hmm. Maybe I'll stay with you. You look a bit like you've been run over."

"Oh, thanks. I'd like to see you in that situation."

"I already told you I was completely impressed. Seriously, though, you've got some gorgeous bruising going on. You look good in purple, but that's got to hurt." He touched her head gently, smoothed away her hair. "Anyway, I have another plan for the afternoon."

"Oh, how mysterious. Are you going to share these plans with me?"

"Depends." Albert sat up. "I'm just going to run out for a minute, get some food and treats. Then we can settle in and recover. You should take one of those pain pills before you tighten up again." He handed her one, which she took with a sip of tea. "Okay, you catch some more sleep. I'll be back before you wake up."

Marian snuggled thankfully down into the covers. She was asleep before she heard the door close.

* * *

It was late afternoon when she awoke after a dreamless sleep. She was so stiff! Groaning, she climbed out of bed and stumbled down the hallway to the washroom. She ran a scorching hot shower and stepped in, rotating her arms and neck under the spray. Gradually the tightness loosened, and she stepped out and looked at her abdomen. Her dressing was soaking wet, and she pulled it off, wincing. She covered the incision with a pad of toilet paper and wrapped herself in a towel. On the way back to her room, she answered way too many questions from the other students. It took forever to get down the hall.

"Wow, are you okay? Sounds terrifying!"

"What did you do? Did they catch the guy?"

"Weren't you scared?"

"I've been praying for you."

"I'm doing a novena." Beth was always so competitive.

Marian waved them all away, pointing to her head, the bruise spreading down her cheek.

"Oh that must hurt. Come on, everyone, let her get some rest. Can we bring you anything?"

Marian smiled at her rescuer and shook her head no, her mind empty, not wanting to engage. Maybe she'd try a novena herself, she thought. Couldn't hurt. And those women at the Compass program sure could use her prayers.

She'd just pulled on a sweatshirt and some yoga pants when she heard a knock on her door. "Dammit," she muttered. "Why can't they just leave me alone?"

It was Albert. He offered her a milk chocolate bar the size of her arm. "Strengthening medicine," he said. "Better for you than the alcoholic kind, I've always thought."

Marian broke off the end, let the square melt over her tongue. Oh, wonderful world that has such things in it, she thought. Chocolate was a magnificent thing. She tried to say thanks but the milky goodness still covered her mouth. So she smiled with her lips shut and gave Albert a hug.

When she stepped back, she noticed Albert was staring at her oddly. "What?"

"You know I could have lost you yesterday, right? He could have killed you."

"I know. I'm trying not to think about it, but it isn't easy when everyone keeps praying for me. Plus, I am starting to ooze. I think I need to put on a new bandage. The shower felt great, but the tape didn't hold."

"Oh, let me. I was a boy scout myself, once." He dug into the paper bag the hospital provided and pulled out a huge bandage and two rolls of paper tape. "Seems a bit of overkill?"

Marian lifted up the sweatshirt and they looked at the cut. It was bigger than they'd thought the night before.

"Wow." Albert gently re-applied the bulky pressure bandage, and they worked together to stick lots of tape on to her abdomen to hold it in place. Marian couldn't stop giggling, which made it all take a long time. Finally, it was done, and she tugged her sweatshirt over the bandage, bent to test the attachment. She pulled another chunk off the chocolate bar and snapped it in half, offering a square to Albert.

Albert swallowed it and licked his lips. "Marian, I need to ask you something. How are you feeling about relationships today?"

"Relationships?" She waved the bar at him. "Well, I'm completely in love with chocolate…" Marian said, but Albert didn't immediately reply. His face looked very serious. "What's up, Albert?"

Suddenly, he swooped into a grandiose kneeling position, swung his arms out. "Dearest Marian, wouldst thou please marry me?"

Marian laughed, stroked his head. "Sweet, I told you. I'm already married. There are laws against that sort of thing."

Albert's face fell. He slumped dramatically, head on her knee, pantomiming sobbing. "But what about us? I need you!" He looked up at her, his face serious again. "I can't let you run off being a superwoman, which I am sure you'll do again, if they won't let me visit you in the hospital. They wouldn't tell me anything about how you were, this time. They kept asking me if I was a spouse or family member. It was awful. I was going to lie, but," he looked right and left, "they don't like that here."

There was a longish, thoughtful pause.

"Okay. I really hate the thought of contacting Neil, but, if I can get a divorce, yes?"

"Really? You'll marry me?" His head poked up, eyes brightening with hope.

"Really. I will. I do love you."

"Are you positive? After all," he said, "you'll be naught but a poor parson's wife."

"You've decided to be a parson?" Marian gazed at him, mouth open.

Albert nodded. "The idea kind of grew on me when I was out with those protests. I said some meaningful things. I was able to stand in front of the crowd, get them calmed down. Even got them to work with the police cleaning up after a protest. Seemed like I could have something to say, might be able to help. Plus, there's the whole 'called by God' thing. I'm getting some celestial nagging." He paused. "Or maybe my parents have worn me down. I don't know, but I think I'd like to give it a try."

"Wow. That's a switch! Are you planning to move back to Shelburne? And, hey! Since when did you read Austen?"

"No, I still can't contemplate Shelburne. But at least I might be able to beg a guest homily or two, make my mum smile."

"But what about the Austen? Didn't someone once say, 'Real men don't read Austen'?"

"I confess, I thought that way myself. Might even have said it. But I saw you had *Pride and Prejudice* on your bookshelf, and I heard about the movie so thought I'd read it, too. Try to impress you. It was surprisingly good. Gave me all sorts of tips. I can toss around additional flowery bits, if you like, if you don't give me a firm answer soon."

"No! Please, no more. Enough! Yes, yes, I've already said yes, I'll marry you! Now, come here."

There was a lengthy tumble of sheets and lips and touches and more. An occasional 'ouch', kissed away. Merry laughter.

Later, Albert leaned up on his elbow and gazed into Marian's eyes. "So, what changed your mind? Last time you were all 'never again,' like you'd been married a hundred times."

She snuggled under his arm. "Nope, just that one marriage, and you know that almost killed me. I vaguely remember hearing about other bad marriages, too. So grateful they weren't mine. Overall, I think I might prefer living in sin. It allows an easier escape and seems appropriately wicked." She shook her head. "I want to be with you, though, and your churchy folks might not agree about the 'appropriate wickedness' part." She held Albert's hand. "Are you sure you are up for damaged goods? I'm probably not worth as much as a new virgin around here."

Albert answered without words.

She detangled. "Well, I'm willing to risk it if you are. But remember, I still have to get through meeting up with Neil and all that. I could skip that drama quite easily. He is a pretty scary guy. Please tell me you want me to go back to 'never again'?"

"No, no, no. You promised. I was curious what caused you to change your mind, that's all."

"I'm not sure—things seem different today. Maybe it was the fight at Compass. I felt so powerful when I stood up and faced that monster. Like for a change I was in charge, not hiding in the back. Even if I did get beaten up. Plus, life seems short all of a sudden, and dangerous. We've got to grab what joy we can. After all, it's the only life we've got. Add whatever other platitudes you'd like me to say." She stretched, moaned, then pulled Alfred into a hug. Releasing him, she added, "Really, though, the other day I had this feeling that you were the person I tried to find for a very long time. You felt right, somehow. Like we were supposed to be together."

"Funny. That's how I felt about you, right when you came in the door of our first class. I thought, 'there she is,' and I knew. I was so scared I'd scare you away."

"Well, we are obviously star-aligned. Meant to be."

"Maybe because we knew each other in a former life? Like when you were Mary, Queen of Scots. And I was a king. Or Sir Francis Drake. Someone famous, anyway."

"As was, apparently, everyone else who reincarnated." Marian laughed. "You'd better not talk like that or they'll throw us out for sure. Live, die, eternity, remember? No do-overs. Especially in the church."

"Unless you're special, like what's-his-name…"

"Well, yes or his Blessed Virgin mum, but you've got to have special connections for that. I wonder if our diplomas would act as a reference. It seems only fair. And I'm not sure I like the idea of eternal heaven, anyway. Altogether too much singing, as Mark Twain would say. Maybe we should join the Buddhists and aim for reincarnation?"

"You are such a heathen!"

"Me? What about you?"

"Heathens both then. You are aware you are the love of my life, right?" Albert said softly.

"Of course. And you, the love of mine."

* * *

Afterword

A word about names. I've tried to stay close to the names that might have been used in each time period (anglicized versions), without causing too much confusion. In modern day I've used Jesus instead of Yeshua for clarity. It can all be confusing and I hope I've got it right…

Some of the first readers of this book wanted to know what happened to Miryam and Daniel in the end. Well, we don't know, do we? Is there a heaven? Can people be kept there for eternity? They, and Peter, each had tasks to perform that involved them stepping into a path of danger, taking the lead, standing up for what they believed instead of just letting others take the heat. Perhaps after finishing these tasks, their reincarnations were over. Perhaps they were reincarnated somewhere else. I do hope, wherever they went, they are happy and together there.

Diane Schoemperlen's charming book, *Our Lady of The Lost and Found* is a different view of Mary, picturing her as traveling all over the world and making appearances. Ms. Schoemperlen has no responsibility for anything in this book, and I mention her only because I loved her novel so very much. You can reach her at: https://www.harpercollins.ca/author/ cr-100026/diane-schoemperlen/

If you have an opinion on this book, it would really help me if you wrote a review.

You can reach me through Somewhat Grumpy Press:
    https://www.somewhatgrumpypress.com
    dorothyanne@somewhatgrumpypress.com

You can connect with me on:
    https://dorothyanneb.com
    https://twitter.com/Dabble58
    https://www.facebook.com/dorothyanneb

About the Author

Embroidery and photo by the author, from painting by Johann Melchior Georg Schmittdner, c. 1700. https://udayton.edu/imri/mary/u/untier-of-knots.php

DA Brown is a retired nurse, writer, artist, and woman struggling with faith. She's been published for over twenty-five years in a variety of venues, including *Army Times*, *Country Connection*, *Ottawa Citizen*, and the *Canadian Author's Association Anthology*. This is her first novel.

An earlier version of this story was shortlisted in the 3DayNovel contest and the Quattro Books Ken Klonsky Novella contest.

www.ingramcontent.com/pod-product-compliance
Lightning Source LLC
Chambersburg PA
CBHW032002180726

48283CB00008B/2539